Tangled In A Lover's Web 3

Dawg vs. Travis

Smoking Web
(BOOK 5)

B'SHONE

ISBN: 978-1-5136-6213-8 (paperback)

Tangled in a Lover's Web Series

Tangled in a Lover's Web Part 1 (Book 1)
B'SHONE & CHINA

How It All Starts
(Book 2) Prequel 1
B'SHONE

LACY: Caviar to Collard Greens
(Book 3) Prequel 2
CHINA

Tangled in a Lover's Web Part 2: Collapsed Web
(Book 4)
B'SHONE & CHINA

FOREWORD

All authors know how to write, but very few have mastered the art of bringing their characters to life.

When I first read B'Shone's novel *Tangled in a Lover's Web Part 1,* I was taken aback by how easily I was engulfed in his book. It made me want to read more of his books, and I am glad I did. Once I read several of his novels, it was easy for me to realize that B'Shone was an expert at bringing his characters to life. Simply put, he writes masterpieces. Readers can be certain that from page one to the end of each of his stories, they will be taken on an unforgettable journey.

I can confidently say that any book written by this amazing author will be so enjoyable that no reader will be able to put it down.

B'Shone's trio of novels appropriately titled *Tangled in a Lover's* Web, and the accompanying set of prequels will hold true to the series name. The novels will twist your emotions and tangle them in the drama-filled lives of the characters. The Tangled in a Lover's Web Series is definitely one to remember.

Daja Alexander

Devil's Don't Die
Dicmatized
Limitless Love

ACKNOWLEDGMENTS

This the 5th and Final book in the *Tangled in a Lover's Web* series. My God! It has been quite a journey, and I am so very grateful for the creative talents that I was blessed with. If it were not for God pouring stories into me, I would not be able to share them with the world, and I am humbled by that blessing.

After typing the final period at the end of the "Tangled" series, I am a little sad because I have been writing about the same characters for over a year and a half now. They became family to me, actually, some of them are my family members. But that's another story. LOL! I will miss writing about Travis, Luther, Lacy, Victoria, Tresha, Dawg, and Malaysia. Their stories captivated readers all over the world, and I am proud to have been able to share them with readers.

As you read *Dawg vs. Travis: Smoking Web,* I know you will be blown away by some of the plot twists I threw into this last installment. I hope I don't make you too mad, but hey, writers do that sometimes. LOL! In this last book, some of the characters quickly find out that life doesn't always have a fairytale ending. I tried to carefully craft an ending that readers will never forget, and I hope you will close this series with a satisfied smile on your face. If not, DM me at my IG handle below and tell me what you didn't like or didn't understand. I love to talk about my books in detail, so I will be happy to hear from you.

To my co-author and the Penhandler's Ink Editing Dept., the Hyde Park Ink Team, and all of my friends, family members, church members, and social media followers, I would be remiss in not acknowledging you. You have supported this series in every way. You purchased paperback books, downloaded e-books, shared our promotional posts, showed up for book signings, and told somebody that told somebody else about how you enjoyed the books. Words cannot express my gratitude. So, I will simply say… Thank you! Thank you! Thank you!

PS: The "spiders" may no longer be in the web; however, I am still writing. Remember to follow me on IG and be on the lookout for more "plot-twisted" tales. Ya' boy got even more tricks up his sleeve. LOL! I'm versatile too, so watch what I release to the world next. Stay Tuned!

Happy Reading,

B'Shone
Natural Born "Penhandler"
IG: @bshone_da_author

TABLE OF CONTENTS

PROLOGUE

The Hospital

Tears streamed down Luther's face as he struggled to say, "Mama."

Travis leaned over to listen, "What you say, lil bruh? I'm here," at that moment, Kesha walked into the room and went to Luther's bed to kiss him on his forehead. She had always been there for the Stewarts. She too, had genuine love for Luther.

He started coughing uncontrollably and struggled to say something, but he didn't say 'mama' again, this time, he said, "granny". He reached for his heart as the cardiac monitor flatlined. Travis and Kesha both screamed for the doctor. Victoria had gotten halfway down the hallway when she heard someone calling code blue and Luther's room number over the intercom system. She tried to maintain her icy exterior and hatred for her husband, but she couldn't. Victoria turned on her heels and almost tripped over her own feet as she hightailed it back to his room. On the way, she looked up and said, "Lord, Please don't take him. Please. I didn't mean any of the stuff I said. I'm so sorry," she screamed in tears and tried to outrun the nurses.

When she made it to the room, she saw Travis arguing with them to allow him to stay while they tried to shock Luther back into the land of the living. Travis won the argument and remained in the room. When he saw Victoria standing at the door about to faint, he made it to her just in time to catch the baby. She almost dropped Laura-Anne as she struggled to hold herself up.

Over and over again, they heard the doctor yell, "CLEAR", but the screen continued to flatline. They watched in horror as the doctors and nurses worked diligently to resuscitate Luther, but after they heard one last "CLEAR". The flatline was permanent.

"Time of death, 3:48 PM," the doctor announced and left the room.

"Aghhh! Aghhh!" Victoria screamed and dropped to her knees. Laura-Anne was torn from her peaceful rest and started crying right along with her mother.

Elizabeth Walker arrived in the ICU at the exact moment that Luther was pronounced dead. She knew where his room was because she heard her daughter screaming as soon as she got off the elevator. She cut the corner and saw her daughter on her knees shamelessly screaming, and the baby was crying just as loud. She also saw Travis standing nearby silently crying and watching the nurses pull the white sheet over his brother's face.

Chapter 1

UNTIL WE MEET AGAIN

The black limousines from MJ Edwards Funeral Home were lined up on both sides of Hyde Park. Everybody that was part of Luther's life growing up was in attendance. People came from everywhere to witness the home-going of one of the pillars of the community. He was known for giving back to the less fortunate, and he selflessly gave scholarships to any child from his neighborhood that had the drive and ambition to go to school to better themselves. Luther had been changing lives in the Hyde Park community for over twelve years, and because of him, there were hundreds of families that were able to move on to bigger and better things. Despite his over-the-top way of living: fancy cars, expensive clothes, high-priced jewelry, and multiple women; he was truly loved.

The funeral director assembled everyone, as they proceeded to Temple of Holiness for the funeral. They all followed each other up Springdale St. and made a left on Jackson Ave. Travis lagged behind in his own car and never turned his emergency flashers on. He refused to ride in a limousine filled with talk about his brother. He didn't want to hear everyone crying and talking about how good or bad Luther was. He just wanted to think of how he was going to avenge his brother's death. Rage entered his heart as he drove past the funeral procession and saw Lacy staring out the window in a daze. Travis knew she would have to be the one to get him close enough to Dawg to pull the trigger. And little did Lacy know, if she didn't lead him to their brother's murderer, he was going to kill her without a second thought. Luther was all Travis knew; he had been the only close family he had since his granny died. He was out for blood.

Lacy looked up and saw Travis staring at her oddly. She mouthed, "Bruh, I'm so sorry."

Unfortunately for Lacy, he wasn't in the mood for any apologies. She was just as in the wrong as her boyfriend. She too did some things that he didn't agree with. He hadn't forgotten that she had kidnapped his child. If she wanted to be in his good graces, she needed to figure out which side she was going to be on and fast. She had a choice between family, or the nigga that killed her little brother. Either way, she had a choice to make, and her time was running out.

Travis nodded his head up and down and mouthed back at her, "But, I'ma kill ya' nigga," Lacy continued to watch her twin with a fearful gaze. She had never witnessed someone without a heart before, so Travis was the first. He wanted Dawg dead so bad that he was willing to kill everyone in his path to do it. She would often ask herself, 'Was this the family she had been yearning for?' She loved her twin, but she was also in love with her little brother's murderer' Dawg. What could she say? Her man was just as heartless as her brother.

Temple of Holiness

One by one, each limo pulled up to the front of the church and allowed everyone to exit and proceed into the church. Several of the men stood outside smoking while waiting for others to arrive.

"I can't believe Dawg shot Dre' in the back," Rick Rude said in disbelief while slowly shaking his head, "It's got to be more to that story than that. Trap and Dawg, them niggas like brothers. Fuck that, they IS brothers. I just don't get it," he turned his back and pulled his emotions together. He didn't want to cry in front of his boys, "A war is coming. And I can't choose a side."

"Me neither," Lil Black said, "I'ma stay out of this one. This shit fucked up."

As the last limo came to a stop, Travis was seen parking across the street because the small church parking lot was packed. Also, he didn't want to get blocked in just in case he wanted to leave before the funeral was over.

Unbeknownst to Travis and the rest of the funeral attendees, a black BMW with a license plate that read: HPG-DOG, was parked a few houses up the street. Shortly after everyone went into the funeral, a tall man and a young female exited the vehicle. They walked into the church and sat upstairs in the balcony.

From the balcony, they watched as everyone walked around the casket to view Luther's body. No one noticed them sitting upstairs. As they watched, they saw Lacy slowly walking back to her seat after seeing her brother laying in the casket. She was fanning herself, and the thoughts of all the time she spent with Luther were weighing her down. Although they fought all the time, he was still her brother, and she hated to admit it, but she missed him already. In addition to losing one of her brothers, the stress of being in the middle of the Travis and Dawg situation became too much to handle. She fainted.

Lacy's father; Travis Stewart Sr., rushed to her aid. As he picked her up off the floor, she opened her eyes and looked up into the balcony. She noticed the tall man looking down at her with concern. A warm feeling came over her, but little did she know, Travis was watching her every move. He was smart. He knew wherever she was, her man was bound to show up. Instincts caused Travis to follow Lacy's gaze, and when he glared up into the balcony, their eyes met. They watched each other like two male lions ready to fight over their territory. Without hesitation, Travis fought through the crowded church as the man raced down the stairs and out the front doors. As Travis made it to the front door, he saw Dawg running across the parking lot. He knew he could get off a good shot and hit him in his back, but just as he was aiming his gun, the young female came up behind him and put her 45 magnum to Travis' head. He froze in his tracks.

"Lower your hammer, Trap. It don't have to be like this," the familiar voice calmly instructed.

"Tameka?" Travis said, as he turned around, "That's whose side you gon' be on?" Travis looked down the barrel of her gun and leaned in closer to allow the barrel to lay on his forehead. "If you gon' shoot bitch, do it!" he gritted his teeth, "You made a grave mistake choosing to rock with him."

Tameka was known for beating females and shooting males. There wasn't a scary bone in her body. Years ago, Travis and Dawg had witnessed her beating two women with her bare hands. After that, they knew they had to get her on their team. But they waited to see if she would fight a man.

One night at *'Hey Baby'*, a club on Hollywood Blvd., the GD's and Vice Lords got to fighting inside the club, and Dawg noticed a male GD beating Tameka senseless in a corner, but she was taking the beating like he wasn't doing shit. Dawg rushed to her aid and beat the man unconscious. Needless to say, Tameka pulled out her 38 and shot the man in the back and ass. Everyone scattered after that, and she walked out as if nothing happened. At that point, they knew she wasn't scared to bust at anybody that tried her.

"It's not like that, Trap. I just don't want y'all killing each other. We're supposed to be family," she reasoned, "But we out here killin' each other. Trap, at least wait til we put Dre' in the ground."

"He the one help put him there!" Travis shouted, "And you want me to wait!" he didn't move too suddenly because she had her finger on the trigger, and the fact that he knew she was one of the baddest female killers that ran with his crew. At that moment, Lacy exited the funeral and saw Tameka holding a pistol to her brother's head. Without thinking, she crept up behind her and knocked her in the back of her head with her heavy handbag, and when she hit the ground, she stomped her in her back twice.

Lacy stood over Tameka yelling, "Bitch, you bold as fuck! How you gon' show up here and try my family like that? Hoe, I hate you," she spit on Tameka, "You musta' forgot, everybody in Hyde Park knew you were the one in the 'Jungle' the day that muthafucka raped me. Your jealous ass was the one that cut my hair off and left me with that sick bastard!" Lacy kicked her again.

Travis reached down and picked up Tameka's pistol. He looked at his twin and walked off. He was still disgusted with her, and she knew it. She had to do something to get back on his good side, and she knew what needed to be done, however, at that moment, she just couldn't do it. She loved both Travis and Dawg, so she had to find another way. She watched as Travis jumped in his car and drove off. Lacy knew the hunt was on.

Inside Trap's Car

'1, 2, 3, let's go...' Black Youngsta and Moneybagg Yo blasted through Travis' speakers as he searched for Dawg. After his ex-best friend fled the scene, he drove around the city checking every spot he could think of. He rode down on every hitter in the hood trying to get them to give him information about Dawg's whereabouts. Unfortunately for him, they were both equally loved, and no one wanted to get in the middle of their family business. Therefore, all of Hyde Park steered clear of the brewing conflict between the two. However, everyone agreed that Dawg was dead wrong for shooting Luther, but they all knew the story behind the shooting had to be more than what was being told.

"Shit! Where is this nigga?" Travis screamed as he hit the dashboard with his fist repeatedly, "Until we meet again, muthafucka. This shit ain't ova!" tears of hurt, neglect, and frustration, were all balled up into one irreversible feeling of revenge. Someone was going to die, and soon.

Inside Dawg's Car

As the sun began to set, Dawg pulled behind Cypress Jr. High and rolled a blunt. The day was unreal, he never imagined having to attend his little brother's funeral, and then to have to run out because he didn't want to defend himself there, against Travis; his best friend; his ride til the end, day one brother.

"I can't believe this nigga came after me at lil bruh funeral," he fired up the blunt, placed his pistol in his lap, closed his eyes, and took a long pull. Behind Cypress, was his get away from everybody. He only went at night. He could park his car in the dark behind the large green dumpsters and go unnoticed.

"Fuck!" he screamed, "Fuck, fuck, fuck! He wasn't supposed to die!" tears raced down his face, "Now, I got to live with this shit! That's why I told Lacy she could never be a killer! But I didn't kill him! I didn't kill him! Yeah, I shot him, but one of them Korean mu'fuckas finished him off! I did NOT kill him!" Dawg reached under his seat and pulled out a pint of Jack Daniels and turned the bottle up, "And to top it all off, Trap's sister is my woman," he shook his head trying to figure out how he was going to get to Lacy, "If she loves me like she said she does, she's gon' have to choose me over him," he took another sip of Jack and mumbled, "I ain't runnin' from no nigga. Fuck it. Until we meet again."

Life was about to get ugly in North Memphis, and Hyde Park was not a safe place for anyone to be living at that point.

Chapter 2

THE HOOD IS TALKIN'

Travis pulled up on Hyde Park, backed in his granny's driveway, and looked around. He had heard everything that was being said in the hood, and it was time to see who was taking sides. He also wanted to see who was smart enough to stay out of the way. The tint of his Cutlass was so dark that no one could see on the inside of it. People walking by couldn't tell if he was in it or not.

Travis turned the music off and watched the reaction of everybody walking by pointing and talking amongst themselves. His windows were cracked just enough where he heard one guy say, *'I got my money on Trap. That nigga ain't shit to play with.'*

Needless to say, he wasn't impressed with the comment. He hated to have to kill his childhood best friend, however; in his heart, it had to be done. Travis snapped his finger as he reached for his phone to make a call.

"Hey what's up? This Trap," he listened to the voice on the other end, "I'ma take care of you and your situation. But, I'ma need you to get next to someone for me," the person on the other end listened, "Ok, so when they approach you and give you their info, just let me know, and I will take it from there. And you will be set for life. I promise."

After Travis hung up his phone. He went back into deep thought. The way he was feeling, he wasn't in the mood to forgive anyone. Not even the man that was walking up to his car.

"Open the door," he pulled on the passenger side door, "Come on, son," the man begged and reluctantly, Travis hit the unlock button and allowed his father to get in, "I know how you feel, but if you react now, you are bound to make a mistake that might cost you your life son," his father pleaded with him.

"I don't give a fuck!" he cursed, "My granny gone, my dope fiend ass mama gone, and now my lil bruh gone. Do you really think I give a fuck about making a mistake, Nigga?" he eyed his dad and waited for him to respond.

"All I'm saying…" his dad started to explain himself.

Travis stopped him, "And all I'm sayin' is... so fuckin' what? Everything I've loved is gone," he snarled at his dad, "Ain't shit else in the world I love," he paused and looked his father directly in his eyes, "That includes you too. You must've forgot nigga, you a coward. You ran out on me when I was 14! Scared to face your demons. I had to have Big Phil killed to keep us safe, and I was just a petty dope boy with nuts! Where the fuck were you?"

Travis Sr., shook his head in agreeance, but before he could respond, Travis' phone rang, and he picked it up.

"Yeah," he listened, "That was my brother and his wife, Vicki's house. That damn house cursed or some shit. I don't want no parts of it," Travis paused, "Hell, give it to Lacy, she can have it for all I care. I don't give a fuck," he hung up and looked at his father.

"Ok, I deserve everything you said about me," he reached for the door handle, "But I'm that same coward that saved you and Dawg's ass behind the movie theater. I'm that same coward that took a charge for you. I'm that same coward that kept you alive," he stepped out of the car. Before he closed the door, he leaned down and said, "And I'm going to be that same coward that might have to bail you out of a jam again, son," he closed the door and walked around to the other side, "Oh yeah, your brother got a baby on the way, and you got a daughter. So, you do have someone to love and care about. Now let that sink in. We love your selfish ass regardless," Travis Sr. turned and walked away.

Ring... Ring... Ring..., Travis looked down at his phone and frowned at a number he didn't know. Normally, he wouldn't answer, however, something on the inside of him told him to answer it. He pushed the answer button and said, "Yeah, speak."

"Trap, this Tameka. We really need to talk. Please…" Tameka tried to talk.

"Bitch, you put a pistol to my head!" he shouted, "We ain't got shit to talk about! You chose the side you wanted to be on."

"Trap, I ain't on no side. I just don't want y'all to kill each other. We are family, please remember …"

"Bitch, please. If I see you again, you just might get a bullet to the head. The only reason I spared your life was because we were at my lil bruh funeral! And from here on out, I might be gunning at you. You got in the middle of something you shouldn't have. Remember that!" Travis pushed the end button on his phone.

He finally got out of his car and walked up the steps to the front door. As he entered the house, he paused at the front door and remembered the time Luther walked in on him getting head from Kesha. He smiled, and then frowned at the memory. He walked into the kitchen and thought about the time his grandmother told him that she wanted him to take care of his lil brother. Then he thought about the time his lil brother said that he saw their mother on the corner in the cold half-naked, and he gave her all the money he had.

"He was an asshole, but he was my lil asshole," he mumbled to himself as tears trickled down his face. He continued to reminisce about his little brother and was startled when he heard a knocking sound.

Knock... Knock... Knock… Without thinking, Travis' natural instincts kicked in. He quickly reached behind his back and pulled out his 9mm. He then quietly walked to the door and as discreetly as he could, he looked through the peephole. No one was there. He turned to walk back to his room, but the knocking started again. He stood to the side of the door and yelled, "Who is it?"

"Trap," the female voice penetrated the door, "It's me, Kesha," again he looked through the peephole, and this time he saw her face. Cautiously, he opened the door. Travis trusted Kesha, but then again, he didn't. One thing was for sure, he knew she was on his side. She was the one that always tried to keep the peace in their crew. As he opened the door, he noticed that she had a friend with her. It was Kita. He remembered her from the day he and Dawg robbed the Night and Day store when they were teenagers. They were able to get away from the store owner because Kesha and Kita held the door open for them. When the store owner was catching up to them, Kesha tripped him up, and he fell.

"Surprise," Kesha said as she and Kita walked into the house. He allowed them to come in, but he stepped on the porch and looked around before closing the door.

"I don't have no one else with me," Kesha told Travis.

"I was getting ready to shoot through the door," he said while closing the door, "I looked and didn't see you the first time."

"You probably looked when I was tying up my shoe," Kesha turned towards Kita, "I found her ass two days ago in Whitehaven in a trap house. Pills," Kesha shook her head in pity at her friend's addiction, "She know you taught us better than that," she expressed, "Anyway, she heard about me getting hit, and I'm down with you. She know whose side I'm on. You took me in when I didn't have shit. Showed me how to live, and never left me hanging. So, she's gon' bust whoever for me, that means she's bussing for you."

Travis looked at Kita sitting on the couch sipping a peach Red Bull looking like an innocent butterfly. He noticed how she was dressed. She looked like a beautiful tomboy, and he was curious. He walked over to her and rubbed her breast, and she jumped back slightly. He then turned and looked at Kesha as she smiled.

"Yep, Trap. She likes pussy," she laughed, "I know you like a book. I knew you were gon' see by the way she was dressed," again she laughed. However, Travis didn't find anything funny. He was testing her because in his mind, he was trying to see how she was going to be helpful in his situation.

"Y'all can gon' leave. This bitch ain't gon' serve no purpose for me," he stated, "If she can't stand to be touched by a nigga, how the fuck she gon' get close enough to do what I need to be done? And plus, my sister got this nigga's nose wide the fuck open. She the one I need to get to him," Travis walked towards the door, "Kesha, I know you rock with me, but she ain't no good to us in this situation. Thanks for trying."

"Trap," Kita stood up and said, "I just fucked Dawg last week. Right before all this shit happened. He gave me $1500. So... I can get next to him. Trust me," Kita smiled and licked her lips.

Travis thought about everything she said but knew it would be better if Lacy led him to Dawg. He felt that if she wanted to get back in good with the family, she was going to have to make it happen. He knew in his heart, that Lacy knew it as well. His sole mission was to erase Dawg from the face of the Earth or break him to submission. He hated the cards that life had dealt him, but he played his hand to the best of his abilities. Travis also knew that his former friend was a worthy opponent, and ever since the enemy line had been drawn in the sand, one of them had to die.

"I'll call y'all if I need you," he assured them.

"Trap, listen to me," Kita said as she stood up, "He been hanging out at Lil Bob's with Danny Sidney on the low."

"Danny knows what's going on. He was at the funeral too," Travis said, as he made a mental note to remind himself that Danny chose to be on Dawg's side, "Ok. I guess I can use y'all after all. Listen, this what I need for you two to do..."

The three of them sat down together as Travis explained how he wanted his plan to be implemented. He put no trust in no one. However, he knew Kesha well, therefore, he had a little faith in her. But Kita's fate would be decided if and when she crossed him.

"So, let's make this shit happen ASAP," Travis announced, "Keep in mind where I told y'all this nigga is gon' lay low at."

"Say less," Kesha smiled because she was actually excited about the plan, "I hate to do this, but hey," she looked at Travis with lustful eyes, "Shiiit, Trap. You were my first pimp, and the first one to send me on a mission. I remember when you sent me to fuck off Big Phil..."

Travis threw an annoyed look at Kesha, and she interpreted it as: '*You are talking too much,*' she knew that look well, so she shut up.

Kesha glanced at Kita and winked at her, "Bitch, let's show Trap the way you and I get down," Kita looked at Travis, then at Kesha shyly, and declined.

"Girl, I'm on my cycle," she lowered her head in shame.

"I ain't got time for that shit right now anyway," Travis shut down their plans for a threesome and took note of Kita's unwillingness to fuck, "Go on and put that plan to work. Holla back when it's in motion."

The girls got up and went into the kitchen, and Travis' phone buzzed. He didn't notice the number, so he didn't answer. It buzzed again.

Calling the number out in his head, hesitantly; he answered, "Yeah," he listened to the strange voice for a minute, until he realized who it was, then he responded, "There is nothing nobody can tell me. I'm gon' do what I gotta do. You can't change my mind! Captain Reid, I fuck with you, this you know. I've done a lot of dirt for you, this you know. So rather than you tryna talk me outta this. Let's focus on what I need. I'ma need a favor from you when this shit go down. If I get jammed, I want out. Or if I get killed, I don't want Dawg in jail. Let him go," again, he listened to Captain Reid speak, "When it's my time, it's my time. I ain't scared to die. My folks gone," he continued to listen, "You sound like that sorry ass dad of mine. My kid and my brother's baby will be just fine," he hung up the phone and went outside and got in his car.

When Travis saw one of Dawg's cars driving by and slow down in front of him, he quickly reached for his pistol. He knew he was being hunted, but he didn't expect for Dawg to be so bold as to bring the fight to his grandmother's house. Travis jumped out and left the door open as he made his way to the back of his car. He tried to take cover, but he was distracted by two men jumping out of Dawg's car.

"Trap!" one man yelled with his pistol in his waist and his hands up, "This Rick Rude, fam!" Rick Rude was Dawg's cousin, and if Travis knew one thing, family always stuck together.

"I just want to talk, fam," Travis noticed that Rick had his gun, but the other man he didn't know. He wasn't taking any chances. He looked over his shoulder because he heard a noise coming from behind him. He quickly turned around, only to be looking at the barrel of a gun that was being aimed at his uninvited guests. Kesha had his back, as usual.

"Ok, I'ma shoot Rick, you take out the other guy," Kesha said, as she squatted down beside him, "I heard the commotion as we was about to head out the back door."

Travis shook his head to let her know he was down with her plan. He then asked, "Where the fuck is Kita?"

"She still behind the house, she ain't strapped."

Travis had a strange look on his face. However, he didn't have time to think about her, "He said he wanted to talk. Just watch my back," he ordered.

"Fo' sho'," Kesha assured him.

Travis stood up and called out to Rick, "Toss your gun in the car, and tell that nigga you got with you to drive off before I unload on his ass."

"Trap, that's my lil cousin. He's only 16, fam. He ain't with the shit!" Rick Rude yelled back.

"I don't give a fuck if he's 6! Either that lil muthafucka move, or if it goes down, I'm killin' him first. His blood will be on your hands, Rude! Make a choice!"

Rick knew that Travis was not playing any games, and if they remained in the stand-off position for too long, someone on the block was going to come out blazing, especially if they thought that Travis was in trouble. Every dope boy on the "shawt-end" of Hyde Park worked for Travis. Rick was lucky that none of them were outside that evening. Everyone was downtown on Riverside Dr. at the Memphis in May festival. Beale Street and Martin Luther King Park were also packed. It was that time of the year, however, for Travis, it was time to live or die. And living through the night was the only thing on his mind. Rick told his little cousin to drive down the street until he signaled for him to come back.

With his hands high above his head, Rick walked towards Travis, "I'm coming up fam," Rick shouted.

"Kesha, keep your eyes on the backyard. I don't trust nobody."
"Kita back there. She'll tell us when someone coming."

"Bitch, I just told you I don't trust nobody! Especially not her!" Kesha shut up and turned around to watch the backyard. Rick walked up and stood in front of Travis. Travis motioned for Kesha to pat him down, and make sure that he didn't have any more weapons on him.

"He clean, Trap," she said when she finished.

"What's up, Slick Rick?"

"Fam," Rick stuck his hand out for Travis to shake it, but he didn't. Rick shrugged his shoulders and started talking, "Trap, my cousin don't want a war with you. Man, he fucked up. He told me it was over TT. A bitch he fucked years ago," Rick calmly revealed, "A piece of pussy will always destroy a nigga. But make that nigga pay for it out his pocket. Don't kill him or make him kill you. We family for real, Trap."

"Nigga, we ain't family! Not no mo'," Travis shouted as he walked up in Rick Rude's face, "That nigga killed my family, over some ass! And you stand here tryna tell me that we family! Nigga, is you for real?" Travis was aggravated, "Bruh, get the fuck out of here! Please, Rick. Stay the fuck away from down here. Because next time, I'ma shoot first and ask no fuckin' questions at all. I fucks with you, but I know you rock with your REAL family! Gon' leave, bruh. You got less than 3 minutes to get off the block!"

Rick Rude decided to walk away. He knew Travis was right. But it was killing him to see two brothers at war over bullshit. He knew in his heart that when the smoke cleared, either Travis was going to need a toe tag or his little cousin; Dawg, was going to need one. Whichever way it ended; it was going to be a sad day for Hyde Park.

Chapter 3

CHOOSING SIDES

Lacy pulled into the Peabody Hotel garage and walked to a private elevator that led to the top floor. As she stepped off the elevator, she dug into her purse for the room key, and accidently bumped into a beautiful young lady that seemed to be coming from her room. However, she could not determine whether she was or not, but she was extremely close to her door.

"Oh, excuse me ma'am," Lacy apologized for bumping into her.

"No, you're fine," she stared at Lacy lustfully.

Lacy finally got her key out and said, "I was digging for this," she held the key up, but when she looked at her door, she frowned, "Did you just come out of here?"

"Oh no, my friend is in the room next door," she giggled and pointed to the room. She then eyed Lacy lustfully, "Anyway, I gots to go," licking her lips, she said, "Hope I can bump," she swayed her hips to the side, "Into you again. I'm always drinking in the lobby. Come down and drink with me sometimes. Have a good day."

Lacy thought the woman was odd, so she smirked at her and nodded ok. She swiped the key across the digital keypad and the green light came on, indicating that she could enter. As she entered the room, she noticed the messy sheets on the bed and frowned. Something was wrong because she knew the bed had been made up before she left that morning. She walked into the restroom and saw Dawg stepping into the shower. Without saying anything to him, she walked back into the room and sniffed the air. She cut her eyes at the bathroom door and took note of the distinct smell of Glade

Blue Odyssey air freshener. Her blood started boiling because she knew that Dawg only used that scent after they had sex.

"Why is he spraying that shit in this room...IF...he was in here by himself? I have been gone all day, so I for damn sure ain't had sex with his ass!" Lacy started inhaling and exhaling to calm herself down, but she couldn't get her feelings under control. After counting down from ten, she gave up on controlling her anger and ran back into the bathroom.

"Dawg!" she screamed, "I know damn well you didn't just have some bitch up in this fuckin' room?"

He stuck his head out of the shower and asked, "Whatchu' say? I didn't hear you baby girl."

"Nigga, did you just have a bitch in this fuckin' room?" she got directly in his face, "Can you hear me now?"

Dawg laughed and kept lathering soap on his body, "Now you know damn well I ain't had nobody in this room, and you got a key."

Lacy wasn't buying it.

"Ok," she stormed out of the room and went next door. She knocked on the door loudly, and eventually a lady answered with a confused look on her face.

"I'm sorry, but did a young lady standing about 5'2, wearing a red mini skirt, and a red and white tank top just come from your room?"

Frowning, the lady said, "Yes. Why?"

Lacy went into her purse and gave the woman a fifty-dollar bill, "She dropped this on the floor, and when I saw it, I tried to catch her, but it was too late."

Still looking confused, the lady took the money and started to close the door, "Ok, I'll be sure...she...gets it."

"Thanks, and I'm sorry to have knocked so hard. I didn't think you would hear me with the loud music," as the lady closed the door, Lacy got a look at the shirt the woman had on. It was a Victor's Cecret shirt, and there weren't too many people in Memphis that were wearing them. The shirts were exclusive to the Hyde Park neighborhood. If you were wearing one, and you weren't with a certain crew, you would catch a severe beat down.

An eerie feeling hit Lacy in the pit of her stomach, and she thought about Dawg.

"That crazy ass sister of theirs still don't know who I am. This is gon' be easy," the lady that answered the door said to someone in the background a little too loudly because Lacy heard her before the door was completely closed.

"Shit!" she screamed and ran back to her room. She didn't have time to argue with Dawg anymore, she knew she had to get him out of the building A.S.A.P.

When she got to the room, he was leaning over the edge of the bed tying his 95 red Air Max tennis shoes.

"Baby, it's time to go. I think my brother knows you are in this hotel."

"Why you say that?" he stood to his feet and grabbed his pistol and Draco, "Watcha' hear?" he rushed over to the peephole, "You seen some of his goons?"

"No," Lacy sucked her teeth in disgust, "But I noticed how this room was fucked up, and how you sprayed the room before I got here, and how you jumped ya' ass in the shower so fast. But that's not the point. I bumped into ya' side pussy in the hallway, and she looked like your type. So, I took my black ass over there and knocked on the door to see what's up. And the bitch that answered the door looked familiar. She looked like one of my brother's hitters!" she explained.

"Are you sho?"

"I can't be 100, but I'm 99% sure."

"Fuck it! If they come through that door, they die. We will leave around two in the morning. We good. I ain't doin' no fuckin' runnin'. It is what it is. I ain't scared of dying."

Lacy looked at Dawg like he was crazy, "BUT I AM! I don't wanna get caught in the crossfire of this shit!" she started crying, "And I don't wanna lose you... or Trap," Dawg held her in his arms and stroked her back.

"Y'all need to stop this bullshit," she pleaded.

"It's gonna be aight love. I ain't gon' let nothin' happen to you," he assured her, "It's gonna be aight."

2 A.M.

Dawg and Lacy gathered their belongings and stepped into the hallway. When Dawg saw a familiar face stepping off the elevator, he quickly snatched Lacy back into their room. He knew if the female would have seen him that Travis would be on his way.

"Damn, that shit was close," Dawg whispered while looking through the peephole, "That bitch loves Trap's dirty drawers. He can do no wrong in her eyes," he continued to watch her as she passed by his room. Slowly, he eased the door open to see what room she was going in. He watched her as she turned the corner and was out of sight, "Get the bags, we gon' take the stairs. Trap too lazy to walk up the steps," his eyes remained on the corner where the female turned.

Lacy quickly made it to the steps and signaled for Dawg to follow her. With haste, he sprinted towards her, and they ran down the steps as fast as they could. When they made it to the first floor, she stepped out into the lobby to make sure the coast was clear. Surprisingly, the lobby was damn near packed.

"Baby, there are people in the lobby, but I don't think they're my brother's people," Dawg wasn't taking any chances. He folded a jacket over his arm with his pistol concealed under it. If anybody moved the wrong way or walked past him too close, they were going to get shot.

He looked around, took a deep breath and said, "Come on baby. Walk ahead of me. I don't want nothing to happen to you if someone comes after me," Dawg paused and thought for a second, *'If she is on my arm, Trap ain't gon' let nobody hurt her,'* "Wait, let's walk together. He ain't gonna hurt me as long as you around. He loves you. He ain't finna let none of his goons shoot while you wit me."

They made it to Lacy's car, and she drove him to his car. As he got out, his hood mentality kicked in. Something was off. He pulled out his pistol and looked around. Two females came out of the hotel acting like they were drunk and staggering. He knew that trick well because he and Travis used to always get females to act drunk, so they could get close to a mark. He was pretty sure the two women were up to no good, but he wasn't 100% sure. Dawg couldn't get a good look at them to determine if they were a threat to him or not. But something told him to hurry up and get out of the parking lot.

"Drive!" he shouted as he jumped back into Lacy's car.

"What's wrong?" she screamed.

"Lacy! DRIVE!" he ordered.

At that moment, one female started running towards them, while the other one tried to unjam her gun. It was then that Lacy's back window was shot out, "Drive, Drive, Drive!" he yelled. She slammed her foot on the gas pedal and balled out of the parking garage. She hit the curves and corners as if she were a Nascar driver.

"When I tell you to do something, baby just do it like Nike! I ain't got time for the questions! Damn! This shit is real!" he screamed, breathing extremely hard, "If my life is on the line, and you're with me, then so is yours."

"I'm sorry baby, but YOU let someone know you were here," she was emotional, "And those two bitches shooting at us, are the same ones from the room next door. And not to mention, Malaysia's ass was getting off the fucking elevator. What the fuck is she even doing there?" Lacy shot back at him as she sped down Union Ave, turning into the Exxon lot where there was plenty of light, and plenty of police, "Now, tell me who the fuck that young bitch was that you had in our fuckin' room?"

Dawg didn't want to get into a heated conversation with her, so he simply told her that she was a friend from the hood. He knew that Lacy was in love with him, and he was in love with her, however; his main concern was getting her out of harm's way. He scanned their surroundings and decided that it would be best if they went to his house.

He picked up his phone and called his people, he then placed the call on speaker so he could roll the blunt that he had in his pocket. When his people answered, he got right to business, "Cuz, did you get a chance to holla at ol' boy?"

"I tried, but that shit didn't work. Oh yeah, Kesha is on his side. Just want you to know that. So, don't think for one minute she won't shoot ya' ass," Rick Rude explained, "I barely made it off the block. He told me that since me and you are real cousins, he knew I was going to ride with you when it all goes down," at that moment, Dawg took the phone off speaker. He didn't want Lacy to know more than she needed to know. He smiled to himself as he watched her drive because it seemed like she was trying to show him that she chose his side. He knew in his heart that she would tell him if she knew someone was coming after him.

"He also threatened to shoot our lil cuz if he didn't drive off. Fam, Trap pissed about this shit. I think we need to try to make peace, but stay ready," Rick Rude informed.

"I don't know about that making peace shit! But anyway, say less. Go get a few of our hitters and go by my house. Watch it til I get there. I'm on my way," Dawg thought about what Rick said, *"Kesha is on his side,"* he snapped his finger and said to himself, "That's who that was in the parking lot. I gots to kill my girl now. But first I got to be sure that Kita didn't ride with her. If she did, she gon' die too. I'ma kill as many as I can before I leave the city,"

"Say no mo'," Rick Rude hung up.

"Bitch!" Kesha screamed, "What the fuck was that shit? Ya' bitch ass acted like you were going to leave me out there by myself!" she was furious, "Why the fuck didn't you bust at they ass? Why the fuck was I the only one bussin'?"

"My gun got jammed. I'm not going at someone and I can't bust. Bitch is you crazy?"

Slap! Kesha slapped her and placed the pistol to her throat, "Don't you ever disrespect me like that again. And if I find out you didn't do what you were supposed to do, I'ma kill you myself! Do I make my fuckin' self clear, hoe?"

Nervous, and with a shaky voice, she replied, "I got you, Keesh… I put it on his Green Bay hat."

20

Dawg's House

Lacy turned into Dawg's driveway as several men jumped out the bushes with camouflage masks over their faces. Instantly, Lacy stopped her car, reached for the gearshift, and prepared to back up. She knew she was not built for that lifestyle, but her love for Dawg was truly unconditional.

He reached for her right hand, "Stop! Them my people," she looked around her and noticed all of the guys faces as they took off their masks, "I told them to stand guard until we made it into the house."

"Those are YOUR people now? A few weeks ago, they were you AND Trap's people! How the fuck you two gon' divide up all y'all friends?" Lacy cried. She thought back to when she watched Victoria tie a sheet around her neck and smile as she fell backwards over her balcony, "I've lost two people that I've loved since I was a fucking child! I'm sick of losing people to foolishness! And from the looks of things, I'm about to lose one more, if not two!" Lacy reaching her breaking point. She was not used to all of the violence. Although her life had been full of drama, she had to admit she still had a decent life overall. She had inherited a small fortune from her adopted parents and was able to find her real family. The thought of her real family made her feel guilty because Travis was her real family, yet she was driving the "getaway car" for his enemy. Lacy couldn't help but to drop her head in shame. Dawg saw her and wrapped his arms around her. But she pushed him away.

"No! I can't do this anymore. I'm tired of losing the ones I love!" she cried.

"Come on, baby," Dawg tried to console her while looking around nervously, "We can't be out here in the opening. Let's go on the inside and talk."

"No! This shit ends now!" Lacy looked through her purse and found her cell phone. She called her brother and placed him on speaker.

"Twin, what's up?" Travis said. He heard her sniffling, "Why you crying?" he asked out of concern, "Trap, I can't take losing another person I love. I lost the only parents I ever knew to violence, then I lost a mother that I never got to know because of more violence, then Tresha, Victoria, Luther, and because of our crackhead ass daddy, I never knew that the woman who saved me more times than I can count when I lived in Hyde Park, was my real grandmother," again, she broke down crying, "Now, you and Dawg ain't gon' stop until y'all kill each other. When does it stop?"

Travis took a deep breath before saying anything, "Listen, twin. That nigga was my brother. We did everything together," Dawg sat on the side listening and lowered his head as he looked out the passenger window, "We all knew Dre' was stupid, but killing him was the wrong move. He didn't deserve that shit!"

"But, Trap, it wasn't his bullet that killed him…"

"Damn, who side you on? Dawg shouldn't have been shooting at him at all! I don't give a fuck whose bullet killed him!" he screamed, "And he was shooting at him over some high school pussy. A bitch he wasn't even married to! That's some weak ass shit! And he knows it. If he had not shot him, Dre's dumb ass would still be here fuckin' his life up some more!"

"Bruh, when it's your time, it's your time. God knew…" Dawg chimed in and tried to reason with Travis, but he was cut off.

"Wait one fuckin' minute. Are you with that nigga now?" silence penetrated the phone. "Huh?" again nothing "So, you with this nigga, and he killed ya' brother! You bitch!" Lacy cried harder when she heard her twin talk to her that way. He crushed her heart.

"Trap, come on bruh…" Dawg tried to say before he was interrupted again.

"Bitch nigga! Don't ever call me brother. You know, one of us is gon' die soon. And you know I ain't scared!"

"I ain't never been scared either nigga," Dawg calmly stated, "So be it. It is what it is. It's war then nigga!"

"And, Lacy. Forget you ever knew me. I hope you get killed in the muthafuckin' crossfire! You can die with that nigga! You chose your side!" Travis hung up after that warning statement.

Chapter 4

HUSH LITTLE BABY

Malaysia sat in her home rocking baby Laura-Anne to sleep after she had given her a warm bottle. She then placed her onto her shoulders to burp her and started singing a nursery rhyme to soothe her.

"Hush little baby don't say a word, mama's gonna buy you a mockingbird. If that mockingbird won't sing, mama's gonna buy you a diamond ring, and if that diamond ring turns to brass, mama's gonna buy you a looking glass…"

Just as expected, before she could finish the song, Laura-Anne had fallen asleep. As she continued to rock the sleeping child, Malaysia stroked the baby's hair as if she were her own. She loved the little girl's father and mother, so she did her best to love the baby. However, as she laid the child in her crib, she couldn't help but to look at her with a little resentment. She rubbed her flat stomach and thought about the day Travis made her have an abortion. She had been regretting that day ever since. She wanted to be the one that gave him a child, not her sister.

An evil smirk morphed onto her face, as she glared to the sky, "Lord, I know that I'm wrong for feeling like this, but in a strange way, I don't feel no type of way that my sister is gone. Please help me to feel sad or something. Please! Because every time I look at that beautiful lil girl, I hate my sister more and more. Although she's gone," she took a deep breath and prayed, "Lord, I pray that she got herself right with you before she did what she did. Please forgive her…" she paused, "And me too. Help me and forgive her. Amen," she walked out of the room and into the kitchen shaking her head, "I don't know if what I said to God made sense, but I feel better."

23

Malaysia's Diary

"May 29, 2020. Why do I continue to love this man when I know he's too dangerous for me? That question continues to float around in my head. When I left the hospital the day Dre' died. I was done with the Stewart family, but I didn't know that both Dre' and Vickie would die that day. And when I saw Trap at Dre's funeral, he looked so helpless. There he was, a new father, and he didn't really have any help with his child because the mother had killed herself. Needless to say, he is the one true love that I refuse to let go. My love for him is deeper than the ocean itself. So, of course, I stepped in to help take care of my sister's child for the man I love. He never treated me bad to the point where I could hate him. Sure, he made some mistakes when he was younger, but didn't we all? At least he was man enough to tell me why we couldn't really be together. The other women- which I knew about- and the street life were a bit much from time to time. But, what's a girl to do? The sex is sooo good. We could make love, have sex, or just plain fuck, whichever one you prefer to call it. Either way, it always blows my mind! I can't let go. I won't let go. I'ma hold on. That's my man. Damn! Love & Life are funny. Oh well! I love him and all of his craziness! He's mine. I've always known that! I hate that I listened to other people all the time, instead of him. Hell, he told me everything. God knows he could have been clearer though! It's easy to listen to others tell you about the man you love, when he only talks in codes and circles! He was always trying to get me to figure shit out instead of telling me how he truly felt. If it were not for his daughter, he woulda' lost me forever. I was really done the day Luther died! AGHHH! TRAP!!! I love and hate you at the same time!" Malaysia paused and thought about the baby. Her heart was bleeding from the loss of the child she should have kept. She continued to write, *"Lord, something is wrong with me. I can't stop thinking about my unborn baby. Please forgive me for what I did then. And please forgive me for what I'm about to do now."*

Malaysia walked back into the room where the baby was sleeping and stood over her crib. She swayed from side to side as she watched the baby squirming in her sleep. She reached for the baby, then stopped. Malaysia stood back up, "No! Don't do it," she told herself. She then leaned down, picked the baby up, and shook baby Laura-Anne until she woke up crying. She smiled and continued to shake the baby while drowning out her tears. Malaysia's eyes told the story of a nervous, scared, and deranged woman, "No, no, no, noooo!" she screamed.

Let the Chips Fall

Dawg's cousin: Rick Rude, and a few of his partner's sat around smoking blunts and watching some of the guys from the neighborhood play basketball at Gooch Park. They were all supposed to be guarding Dawg to keep the drama down. But more importantly, they were trying to keep innocent blood from filling the streets of Hyde Park.

"What we gon' do?" Rick Rude asked, "We can't let them nigga's kill each other," he explained to the rest of the crew, as he shrugged his shoulders.

"What we need to do is get with some of Trap's hitters and try to bring them two together, without them knowing it," Big Marvin suggested, as he stepped out of his Tahoe, "We ain't got beef with them and they ain't got beef with us. Mane, this shit is crazy as fuck because we bout to be shootin' at niggas that we was just choppin' it up and partyin' with just a few weeks back. We all one crew, now we on opposite sides of the fence because Trap won't listen. It's up to us to fix this shit before it gets out of hand."

"That shit you talkin' sounds good, but we all know how that's gon' end. I went over on Hyde Park and tried to reason with his ass, and he told me to get the fuck off his block!" Rick laughed to himself.

"Yeah, you're right. Sounds good, but them niggas loyal to him," Bird chimed in, "The only way we can fix this shit is if we just don't shoot at them. No retaliation."

Rick stopped smoking and looked at Big Marvin. They both then looked at Bird and fell out laughing.

"Nigga, so we supposed to just LET mu'fuckas shoot at us? Nawww bruh,'" Rick pointed out, "I ain't no gotdamn Superman or nobody. Bullets don't bounce off me. If them niggas shoot at me. I'm shootin' back. Point, blank, period!"

As the basketball game came to an end, several of the players got into an altercation. A fight broke out on the court and pistols were brought into the mix. Big Marvin and Rick ducked behind his Tahoe and some of the guys on the court ran and hid behind them. People were running everywhere. Another guy with his gun in hand ran behind Marvin's Tahoe and looked around the truck.

"I think it's over," Rick Rude said to Marvin as they stood up, "Thank God no one was hit."

"Mane, I hate to tell ya', but two people just got killed out here," a guy informed Rick, as he hid with one of the gunmen. After hearing the sad news, everyone started looking for the bodies.

"Shiiit where?" Rick asked.

"Right there," one of the gunmen pointed to his left. When everyone looked, he put two holes in Big Marvin and Rick Rude's head.

"Two down and four more to go," all three of the guys that stood behind the truck with them smiled, "Great acting fellows. Just like Trap said. Like taking candy from a baby. Now on to Dawg's house to get the others," the gunman looked down at Rick and Marvin's bodies, "I bet them niggas in hell wishin' they woulda chose the right side."

They all jumped into Big Marvin's truck and drove off, "I'ma take the rims. Y'all niggas can have the motor and music," laughter filled the Tahoe as they all said in unison, "Let the Chips Fall."

One Hour Later

Crime scene tape blocked off Gooch Park as word traveled throughout the North Memphis area. Two bodies were found with no sign of drugs or other guns involved.

"Search for anything that they may have left behind. Bullet shells, empty bottles. Anything!" Captain Reid yelled as he looked around. He pointed, "Check that beer bottle over there."

"Yes sir, Captain," a young officer responded.

"And check with some of the people standing around. See if they heard or seen anything. I know they're all gonna say they haven't but check anyway."

At that moment, a homeless man with raggedy jeans, a torn shirt, and shoes that appeared as though they had seen better days, slowly strolled towards the basketball court. He reached down for the beer bottle, but the young officer stopped him. The man was thirsty and wanted something to drink.

"Don't touch that bottle!" the young officer said, as he raced over to it.

The man staggered and looked around, "Hell, why not? Them boys always…leave…" he slurred his words, "some...thing...in the bottle," again he staggered, "For me."

"So, you know the guys that were up here?" "Yeah...Lil Bug...Snake and nem," he said as he got closer to the officer.

The officer stepped back a few feet because the man's odor was offensive, "Do you know their real name? Or where they stay?"

"I...I... ain't no snitch," he said, as he turned and walked off, but quickly stopped, "Give me some money, I might know...one...one...one… of them names. And I want 22 dollars and 13 cents."

The young officer laughed but agreed. He reached in his pocket and discreetly slid him twenty-two dollars, "Now tell me his name and where he stays."

"No suh! I said 13 cents too," the homeless man held out his hand to the officer.

The officer frowned at the man and dug deep into his pocket for a dime and three pennies, "Here," he handed the change to the man, and he accepted with a snaggletooth smile.

"His name...name is Keith. And he live on Clayton. Yep, right at the dead-end. You can't miss it!" the man turned and started walking away.

The young officer raced over to his Captain to tell him that he knew the name of one of the guys that had been on the court playing basketball before the murders. He was excited because he was a rookie on the force and wanted to please his Captain.

Excited and out of breath, he reached the captain, "Okay, Captain, that old homeless man down there by the driveway said that one of the guys on the court's name was Keith, and that he lives on Clayton. And I just gave the beer bottle to forensic to be tagged."

Quickly, the Captain turned around, "Grab that man!" he shouted, "Grab his ass NOW!"

However, it was too late. A car pulled up and the homeless man jumped in the backseat. "Gotdammit!" he screamed at the young officer, "He played yo' naive ass! That had to be Trap! or Travis...or whateva' street name he usin' now! Keith wasn't up here!" he continued to scream, "This is his fuckin' cousin laying here dead! Trap always returns to the scene of the crime. He gets a kick out of this shit! That nigga is sick when it comes to killing!" anger rushed through him like a bolt of lightning as he stared at Rick Rude's body.

"This shit just got real! Dawg ain't gon' like this! First Luther, now Rick. They killin' family members now! I know the bodies about to start droppin' all over the place!" Captain Reid shook his head and finished surveying the crime scene.

Chapter 5

TOO MANY TEARS

Lacy was suddenly drawn out of a restless sleep by the rising temperature in Dawg's room.

"Damn! That thermostat must be set on: HELL! It's hot as fuck in here," she whispered while wiping sweat beads from her forehead. She reached for Dawg, but he wasn't there. She knew where he was because of the loud noise in the house. She got out of bed and washed her face. As she stared at the mirror in the bathroom, she realized that the room was not as hot as she thought. She had been having a nightmare.

Lacy turned on the television to watch FOX 13 morning news, only to see images of Rick Rude and Big Marvin scrolling across the screen. The story was Breaking News. Both men had been killed in Gooch Park. Her hand started to tremble as she thought of the only person that had enough balls and brains to pull something like that off without getting caught. She reached for her remote control and turned the television up louder so she could hear what the reporter was saying.

"What you see behind me, is the aftermath of what was a gruesome scene. It has since been taped off by the Memphis Police Dept. But, from what we have vaguely been told by police and members of the Hyde Park Community, yesterday, around 4 pm, the bodies of the two men you see on the screen were found near the basketball court here at Gooch Park. It is unknown to us at this time the cause of this horrific tragedy. However, it has been reported that the names of the murder victims are two black men: Rick Rainey 51 and Marvin MacAdory 52. Also, we do know that both men were

shot in the back of the head execution style. There is no suspect in custody at this time. Stay tuned to Fox 13 as we bring you more updates on this double homicide. Reporting live, I'm Jenny Jones for Fox 13."

Tears formed in Lacy's eyes. She shook her head in sadness and disgust because she knew it was just a matter of time before her twin brother or the love of her life ended up dead. She walked into the camera room and watched Dawg watching his monitors. Nervously, her hands shook. She walked over to the window, and from somewhere deep inside of her, a familiar melody forced its way through her lips.

"The Itsy-Bitsy Spider went up the water spout. Down came the rain and washed the spider out. Out came the sun and dried up all the rain…" she stopped singing and thought of something she had to do, "I gots to bring this shit to an end. This is driving me crazy. I cannot end up in Lakeside again. I just can't! I don't think I will survive this time," she cried, "I love them both. Lord help me."

Again, the thoughts of Victoria hanging herself from the balcony entered her mind. Lacy knew that she egged her mentally unstable friend along, and the reality of what she did haunted her night and day. She could have prevented her from meeting her demise, but she didn't, and that truth caused more pain to her fragile heart. She remembered what Dawg told her about committing a murder, and how it would eat her alive. He was right. She remembered that she had killed someone before, but that person was trying to rape her. So, she felt no remorse for protecting herself.

"Why didn't I listen to him?" she asked herself, as she walked through the house mumbling incoherently. She was slowly approaching her breaking point. Little did she know, Dawg was watching on the monitor and noticed her hands shaking uncontrollably, as she gazed into space, humming the *Itsy-Bitsy-Spider* song. He wanted to comfort her, but he knew he had to allow her to work through her own issues. He also knew what he would have to do to help her, and there was no way possible that he could fix the problem that he and Travis were having. He tried once, and that was all he was willing to do. However, Dawg was grateful that he warned Lacy of the consequences that would come her way if she rode with him. That eased his conscience a little. Very little.

He continued to watch her every move. She stared out the window blankly, twirled her hair around in circles, and continued humming the nursery rhyme. He was tossing the idea around about letting her go home. He felt that she might be able rest better there. As he watched, she all of a sudden stopped humming and leaned closer to the window. She noticed a masked man creeping around the backside of Dawg's house.

"Baby!" she screamed.

Dawg stopped watching the camera and rushed to the front room.

"What's wrong?" he asked, taking her by the hand.

Nervously, she shook, "There is a masked man trying to ease up the side of the house. And he had a gun. A big one."

"Baby, I been watching the monitors all night. We good. Even Trap ain't crazy enough to try me on my street, in broad daylight. You were daydreaming and you didn't sleep well, that's why I got up. You tossed and turned all night," he pulled her closer to him, "Go home and get some rest. I'll be here. I might be the bigger man and move to Cashville or Dallas, if you come with me. Maybe if I leave Memphis, Trap will let this shit go!"

Lacy was silent. Her mind was on the masked man. She knew what she saw, and she wasn't going to let it go, "Dawg, I'm telling you that there is a masked man roaming around outside somewhere, laying low. I know I'm not street savvy like you and my brother, but I know what I saw. Please listen to me, and call your crew over," she begged.

Dawg took her by the hand and walked back into the surveillance room. He reversed the footage back twenty minutes from the side of the house she was referring to and played it for her. There was no masked man on the camera, "See baby, nobody was there. I told you that you're just sleepy."

Lacy rushed back into the room and put her clothes on. She was ready to go. She knew she wasn't delusional; however, the camera made her feel as though she were, "Maybe you are right. I do need some rest. So I'ma go home and call you later baby."

They kissed, and Dawg walked her to the door. He was prepared to walk her to her car, but she stopped him, "No, baby. I don't see your boys, so I'm good right here. Please go back into the house," he smiled and agreed, but remained on the porch until she got in her car and backed out.

Chapter 6

STRANGE VISION

Dawg sat in his home staring at the surveillance monitors. He had been stuck in that position for days. As he thought about his cousin; Rick Rude, he bit down on his bottom lip to calm the raging beast inside of him. He knew everything stemmed from his actions, and he wanted it to come to an end, however; he had to get even. When he shot at Luther, he only meant to teach him a lesson, he was not aiming to kill. But he knew that Travis purposely killed his cousin in cold blood. He looked to the left of him at a picture of Rick, Travis, and himself.

"Those were the days. Fuck! I shouldn't have shot that lil nigga. Fuck! All over some childhood pussy! And I might lose my life or kill my brother, or even get someone else killed in the process. This shit has to end," he thought about leaving town again, "But then it would seem like I'm the coward," he dismissed the thought, "Nope. I ain't never ran from a nigga in my whole fuckin' life," he continued to try to make excuses to justify his choice not to leave town. However, his love and brotherhood for Travis was bigger than his pride. After thinking for a few more minutes, Dawg's mind was made up, "Yeah, I'll pack up and leave. This will be best for the both of us," he took a deep breath and looked at his home through the monitors. As he scanned every room, he was letting it soak in that he was about to leave everything he ever knew behind. He zoomed the camera in on his downstairs office and glanced at his real estate license, his contractor's license, and the pictures that lined the walls of every building he had ever helped build or sell. He smiled with pride as he thought about how far he had come. He grew up in an abusive household, and until he started hustling with Travis, he sometimes didn't know where his next meal was coming from. Dawg had come a long way in his life, he currently had several homes, cars, and he was worth millions. He also had the love of his life; Lacy. Until the day he shot Luther, he was happier than he had ever been. Unfortunately, he had to face the fact that if he stayed in Memphis, all of his hard work and everything he learned from being in and out of prison would have been in vain.

"Fuck!" he screamed, "I hope Lacy go with me. But first, I got to try to reason with Trap one more time," he picked up the phone and made a call.

"I'ma need you to do what I told you about days ago," he listened to the person on the other end, "I don't care what you think he might do or say. I'm trying to bring this mess to an end. Baby girl, be like Nike, and Just Do It! Don't call me until it's done!" Dawg tried to hang up, but her defeated tone stopped him.

"Dawg, I've called him to talk, but he didn't want to hear it," she revealed weakly.

"Get it done," he screamed into the phone and hung up in her face.

Lacy's Car

Lacy left Dawg's house heading home. Her stomach reminded her that she hadn't eaten since the evening before, so she decided to pull over at the Burger King on Hollywood and I-240. As she turned into the parking lot, she nearly hit a lady walking to her car. Quickly, she slammed on brakes.

"I'm so sorry ma'am," Lacy yelled out of her window, and was shocked when she realized who the lady was. Quickly, she exited her car and walked over to speak, "Erica, is that you?" she asked.

Erica looked up and noticed a woman walking towards her. When she placed the woman's face, she realized that it was her deceased baby daddy's sister. She smiled and turned around, with open arms.

"Hey. I remember your face, but just not the name. You're Luther's sister, right?"

"Yes, Luther is…," Lacy dropped her head, "Was my brother. What are you doing out here eating bad food? Travis told me you were having a boy, so you know my nephew got to get the best food in him. Don't get started with all that junk food," Lacy smiled as she joked with Erica. She looked at Erica's figure, "I know you don't want to mess up that hourglass shape you got."

Erica smirked, but stress wrinkles were all across her forehead, "Girl, I have been eating everything under the sun. I'm sorry I didn't make the funeral. I talked to Travis that day, and I told him that my morning sickness was on 10. He told me that he understood. Truthfully, I couldn't bring myself to see Luther lying in that casket like that. It's gonna be hard for me knowing he is gone. I don't have no kids, so I ain't never been no mama before, and now I gotta raise my first baby without a daddy. I've heard how low down he was to people, and the last time we were together, he was an asshole to me too, but I never wanted anything to happen to him. I knew he would have been a good dad though," she sighed and turned to get in her car, "Anyway, take care…" Erica snapped her fingers to try to remember the name.

"Lacy," Lacy reminded her.

"That's right. I'm sorry. I think I got pregnancy brain or something. I'll remember it from here on out. Lacy. Take care Lacy," Erica tried to close her car door.

"Wait, here is my number. You can call me if you ever wanna talk. And remember…" Lacy took her by the hand, "Trap and I will be with you all the way. He will have a father figure in his life. And my man; Dawg, will help as well. The baby is a Stewart therefore, he's gonna be just fine. It's gonna be alright. I promise," Lacy assured her.

Erica accepted Lacy's phone number, smiled, and drove off. Evil thoughts invaded Erica's mind as she drove, "Some kind of way, I will be a Stewart."

Opportunity had presented itself, and she was about to take full advantage of it. Erica made up her mind that she was going to be a part of the Stewart clan, and her son was going to make sure that she was financially taken care of forever. She was going to get the money she deserved and much more, and Lacy was going to be her way in.

****Lacy's Home****

Lacy wasted no time taking a quick shower and crawling into her king-sized platform bed. She didn't want to talk to anyone. She just wanted to be alone and get some much-needed rest. As soon as she closed her eyes, she drifted into a deep sleep.

The thought of the masked man she thought she saw walking around Dawg's house made her twitch in her sleep. She immediately woke up in a cold sweat and frowned as she tried to envision the masked man.

"I know that man. But it wasn't my twin. I know that man's walk," she said, as she stood up nervously and walked to the bathroom to wash her face, "Damn! I can't even sleep at home either. Aghhh…" she screamed, "I know that masked man," she continued to tell herself, "Or did I really see someone? Maybe I'm trippin'! We checked the cameras and didn't see anybody. Lacy, get it together you. Let it go. You losin' it girl," she admitted to herself and sat on the edge of her bed.

"I guess I'll go over to my new house and clean up a lil bit. I already had it painted, and they brought my new furniture yesterday. All I need to do is put me a few plug-ins in there, light a few candles, let some soft music play and fuck my man tonight," she smiled and tried to push the drama from the previous two weeks out of her mind, "I wonder what Erica is up to. I should call and check on her," she thought, "I'm sure she has been cooped up in the house for days, so maybe she'll want to come over and help me, or just keep me company or something. I can also see where her head is and see if she wants me to hook her up with one of my rich friends," she paused to think to herself, "Yeah, I'ma call Erica. She'll have to do. I don't have any other friends. I might as well make the best of it. Shit, I would like to hang with Malaysia and the baby, but I can't have her and Dawg around each other because I know she'll tell Travis," she rolled her eyes, "I hate this shit! I'm in the middle of this, and I didn't do a damn thing wrong!"

Before Lacy got up to get dressed, her phone rang. It was her brother, Chris. He told her that he wanted to finally have the conversation that the drama from the previous weeks would not allow them to have. She agreed that it was time and told him to meet her at Victoria and Luther's old home on Monteigne Dr.

Lacy changed into a fitted Nike short set and combed her hair. She looked at herself in the mirror and said, "Flawless," she then packed an overnight bag because she knew she wasn't returning to her old house that evening. She had already spoken with Dawg, and he knew what tip she was on. She wanted to relax, lay up with him, and fuck in every room in her new home. But first, she needed to talk to her little brother.

The House on Monteigne Dr.

Chris and Lacy made it to the house at the same time. They walked in and made themselves comfortable in the kitchen and ate junk food while starting their trip down memory lane.

"So, sis, what I am about to tell you is going to blow your mind, but I think you already know some of it. Like... I know you know who my parents are right?" Chris asked.

"Yes. Your parents adopted me illegally as fuck from my biological parents; the Stewarts," Lacy laughed at her crazy past.

"Correct. And of course, you already know what happened to them. Right?"

"All I know is that they were killed at the Embassy Suites off Poplar Ave. But that story always seemed crazy to me."

"Yes, it should have sounded odd because the real story was that our dear sweet aunt Hannah set them up to be killed. After that, she took the insurance policy that belonged to you, threw you in that horrible foster home in North Memphis, and went back to Seattle. Of course, you already know the coronavirus killed her evil ass a few weeks back, so it looks like she got what she deserved."

"Yeah she did! But, none of that explains how you're here right now.

I mean... mama was killed in that hotel room... according to the police report, she was dead on arrival at the hospital. So, how in the hell are you...?" Chris finished her sentence.

"Alive! You wanna know how I'm alive?" Lacy nodded, "Ok... this is what happened. Remember that mama was 9 months pregnant at the time of the triple murder at the hotel. When the paramedics arrived, they immediately rushed her to the hospital, and although she was DOA, the doctors worked miracles and was able to remove a healthy baby boy; ME, from her womb. Just as I was being taken to the hospital's Nursery, our mother's mama; Carol Clark, swooped into the hospital with former mayor; 'Boss' Walker, and he used his clout to change my last name from Blake to Walker. After that, they cremated our mother, and her ashes are on the mantle at your old home in River Oaks. Actually, I was also raised in that house. Papa Walker owned it, so he let his mistress; Carol, and I live in it. He then paid her hush money to keep me; his illegitimate grandson, away from Victoria, Elizabeth, and his wife; Mildred. As time went by, 'Boss Walker' became attached to me, and he spent most of his spare time at my house. He had never had a son before, and he always wanted one. Carol eventually met some man that promised her more than what my grandfather was giving her, so she disappeared. I hate to admit it, but our grandmother was a hoe... for real. Anyway, your former nanny; Ms. Estelle, was hired to look after me, and that is how I found out about you and what happened to our parents," Chris explained while Lacy cried. The trip down memory lane was a rough one for her.

She hugged Chris tightly and cried on his shoulder, "So, you were a miracle baby! My God, I was so excited when mama told me she was having a boy. I wanted a little brother so bad! I'm glad you survived. Well..." she looked away in pain, "I had two little brothers, but Luther just wouldn't act right. I hate to say it, but I miss his ugly ass," she laughed, "Wait a minute... Ms. Estelle raised you? Is she still alive? I wanna go see her, call her for me. I would love to hear her voice." Lacy was excited until the look on her brother's face told her she would never talk to her old nanny again.

"She's dead, isn't she?" Lacy asked and Chris nodded yes.

"She died of cancer a few months ago. She knew you were ok though; she just didn't want to interrupt your life with painful memories of the past. Elizabeth Walker kept her up to date. Also, after she died, I've been pretty much living in the house by myself. I'm 18 so… Anyway, I got the house in Papa Walker's will. I can't wait until you come visit me there. You still have childhood pictures and everything in that house. You'll love it!"

"Good ol' Mama Liz! I need to call and thank her for that. I haven't really checked on her like I should since Vicki killed herself," Lacy looked away in guilt, and her brother knew what was on her mind.

"Lacy, Vicki's death was not your fault. She was a troubled child from what I hear. Papa Walker said she had some sick fixation with spiders, and they always caused her to do crazy stuff. They never knew where her problems stemmed from, so they just dealt with it. Anyway, she has always had a fragile mind, you know that!"

"I know! But I felt so out of place at her funeral. They buried her a few days before Luther," she laughed, "Mane, y'all white folk be burying the dead like 6 hours after y'all die. That shit is crazy!" Chris laughed with her because he was happy to see his sister smiling.

"Ummm, Lacy, remember, Vicki ain't white!" he laughed again.

"You're right, she did have a black daddy!" Lacy got serious, "Chris, where do we go from here?"

"Well, I know that Mr. Durrham gave you your money. So, you should be ok financially. If you need any more just let me know. Vicki, Ms. Elizabeth, and Mrs. Mildred never knew it, but 'Boss' Walker had taken out another life insurance policy just for me. So… let's just say I got plenty of money. For all points and purposes, he was my dad, and I know he was racist, but Ms. Estelle made sure I did not inherit that ignorance."

Lacy cringed every time "Boss Walker's" name came up. She wanted to tell Chris how much of a child molesting, racist asshole his "dad" was, but she didn't want to cause him any undue stress. She simply smiled and allowed him to have his memories in peace.

"Sis, you and I are going to be good. I just need you to start thinking about what you've gotten yourself into with this street mess you're involved in. I mean...you got people chasing you with guns and shit out of hotels and stuff!" Chris revealed.

Lacy looked at her brother in confusion, "How do you know what happened at the hotel with me and Dawg a few days ago?"

Chris smiled, "I just know shit sis," he winked at her, "But anyway, I gotta go! I got a paper due tonight. The U of M professors are still giving us work even though this pandemic is going on. I will call you later," he got up, hugged his sister again and left.

Lacy sat for a moment and thought about everything Chris told to her. After a few more moments of reflection, she decided to leave the past in the past and move forward with her original plan, she called Erica.

Chapter 7

GOTCHA'

Travis had been laying low while putting his plan in motion. He wanted everything to play out the way he put it together. However, he had been in this position more than once, and he knew everything never went according to plan. So, he always had a plan B; a plan on top of a plan. He also knew that there was a strong possibility that he would not come out of the war with his former best friend alive therefore, he had made the necessary arrangements. Lacy would get all of their empire, along with his daughter; Laura-Anne, as well as Luther's son. He had previously worked the details out with Erica, and she went for it. Travis even made sure that Malaysia's future was secure, although he knew she was forever financially taken care of.

"Okay, let me see," he said as he walked to the garage. As he hit the small glowing button on the wall next to the door, the garage came up. To his surprise, Captain Reid, and a couple of officers were standing there with their pistols drawn.

"Luther Stewart, put ya' hands up!" Captain Reid yelled, however; Travis stood there. He knew they didn't have anything on him. And if the Captain didn't leave his house, he was going to have him running for his life.

"Reid, what the fuck do you want?" Travis said, as he picked up a pair of Nike's off the floor of his garage, "I ain't got time for ya' shit today," he turned and walked back towards the door. He looked back, "Are you coming in? Just you...not them two rookies. They can stay their asses out here. And don't touch shit!" Captain Reid walked in behind him.

He looked back at his two officers, "I'll be right back," he walked in and sat at the kitchen table, "I see you living good," the Captain complimented as he admired the home. Travis ignored him.

"Cap, what the fuck do I owe the pleasure of you being in my muthafuckin' house?"

Captain Reid laughed, "Why the hostility? You're not glad to see an old friend?"

"I ain't never been friends with a pig."

Again, the Captain laughed, "We were friends when I got rid of all that evidence on those two murder charges. I was your friend, when Dawg shot Lil Black, and I made that shit disappear. I was your friend then. But now we ain't friends?"

"Look, Cap. I got shit to do. So, what the fuck do you want?"

"You one cocky muthafucka' Stewart. But I got ya' ass now. We don't owe each other anymore favors. I know you killed those two men at Gooch Park," he paused for effect, "See, they had cameras installed around the top of the pool entrance. And as soon as they clear the footage, your black ass is going away for a long time. See, you thought I forgot about you killing my cousin; Big Phil," again, he paused, "But payback is finally here! And I will have the last laugh."

Travis took a deep breath, "The way I see it. You don't have shit on me because if you did, I would be in jail right now. And if I were, I wouldn't be there long because you was gon' get me off," he responded arrogantly.

Captain Reid bolted to his feet, "How the fuck you figure that?" he slammed his fist on the table, "Listen to me nigga! Yo' black ass is goin' down this time!"

"Captain," Travis was calm, "You ain't gon' do shit. And if you even think about coming for me, I'ma make you regret the day you ever crossed me," Travis walked over to the fridge and took two bottle waters out. He glanced at his sugar and flour bowls and straightened them up. He then turned the lid on the flour bowl making sure it was turned around correctly. He was a neat freak, "Drink one and calm your fat ass down," he sat one of the bottles of water on the table, "I didn't kill those two guys. I'm a law-abiding citizen and shit, Captain," he smirked, "Now, maybe I know who did, but you know I ain't ya' snitch. So, fuck you, before you ask me."

"I got so much shit on you that your baby will be a grandmother before you get out. You'll die behind bars if I got something to do with it. I'm done covering up your shit."

"No, you're not. You stupid muthafucka'. You came over to my house and just admitted that you covered up some murders for me, so that makes you an accomplice," Travis turned and pointed to a small camera that was meticulously placed on the flour bowl. It was aimed at the kitchen table, "Smile, you're on candid camera. And I recorded it on my phone, which is saved in I-Cloud. I'm smarter than your average thug, Fat Boy. Gotcha'."

Reid rushed over to the flour bowl and looked in, "You muthafucka' you! I ought to kill you right now! You sonofabitch! You set me up!"

"You set your own ass up," Travis laughed, "Now who's laughing? You came over to MY house," he shook his head at the Captain in pity, "You're slippin' man! I think it's time for you to retire! You should have left me alone. But no. Now you will be my bitch forever," he paused, "I'm just playin', Cap. You my nigga. I ain't no snitch. I'll kill you before I snitch on you," the Captain didn't know that Travis had the remote to the camera in his hand. He paused it before he said, *I'll Kill You.*

"You're threatening an officer!" he yelled, "Fuck ya'! I'ma do my job, nigga!"

"And I will do mine. Now, see your way out. I gots to go do my job," he paused the camera, "Kill me a couple of cops," he laughed, as he went into his garage. He looked back at Captain Reid, "Come on, Fat Boy. It's time to go," hesitantly, Reid walked out and whispered to Travis.

"I'ma kill you before Dawg. I promise you that one. Now you got two niggas after you."

"Oh well, take a number and get in line," Travis jumped into his new F-350 and pulled off as his garage door went down. Captain Reid was pissed because he knew he had just put himself in a bad situation. He knew his life was in the hands of a thug, and he didn't like it one bit. He had to get Travis out the way.

Reid remained in Travis' driveway as he watched his taillights turn the corner, "That nigga gon' die soon," he mumbled to himself.

"Who's gonna die, Cap?" the Rookie officer asked. Captain Reid looked at him as if he wanted to slap the fuck out of him. He knew damn well who he was talking about.

"Get in the fuckin' car and drive!" he yelled, "Don't ask me no fuckin' questions. Just drive!"

Chapter 8

TRAP GONE WRONG

Travis pulled up in front of his grandmother's house and rushed inside. He still wasn't comfortable enough to hang out on the block just yet, although he knew Dawg truly didn't want a war. He still had to be cautious. Travis loved Dawg, but the sting of him shooting his little brother was still burning on the inside.

As he entered the house, he looked back and noticed Kita coming up the street. There were two young guys behind her staring at her ass. Travis laughed to himself because he knew they were trying to convince her to give them some pussy for some Percocet 30.

Travis did his research on Kita the day Kesha told him that he found her in a trap house in Whitehaven. And, when she said that she fucked Dawg, he knew what time it was with her. That's all Dawg sold. Perc 30. Just as Kesha said, Kita was a "pill head". He tried to use that in his favor. But something went wrong. He wanted to know what transpired that night at the Peabody hotel. He waited until she made it to the front of his granny's house and signaled for her to come in. She smiled because she thought Travis wanted to fuck her. She happily skipped up the steps and into the house.

He slammed the door behind her, and wasted no time questioning her.

"What the fuck happened at the Peabody? I told you the room number," he walked up on Kita, grabbed her around the throat, and squeezed as hard as he could. He was purposely trying to make her stop breathing. Calmly, he spoke through gritted teeth, "I told you to fuck him. And I told you to kill that nigga while in the room. What the fuck happened?" Travis had gotten agitated. The plan was perfect. But somehow, it got messed up, and he wanted to know how. He let her go and shouted, "Talk, bitch!" he pulled out his 9mm and placed it to her head, "Or I'ma leave your brains splattered all over this living room!"

Kita bent over grabbing her throat and trying to catch her breath. She looked up at Travis in fear for her life. She didn't know what to say. She was too scared to tell him the truth and too smart to lie. She looked up at Travis again.

"Trap, I got in the room and we started talking. We drank some wine…" she said nervously. Again, she rubbed her throat. He had left visible fingerprints on it, "We laid back in the bed, and he started taking off my clothes, but he looked at his watch and stopped. He panicked and said, '*Oh shit, my girl on her way back*', he jumped up and started spraying the room. Then he took a shower. That's it! That's what happened in the room. I promise!" she backed away from Travis slowly. She could tell by the look on his face that he knew she was lying.

"So, what you're telling me is that you were only in there for about 5 to 10 minutes right?" he calmly asked, as he took a seat on the couch.

"That's right, Trap. Bout…" she thought for a second, as she looked at the door realizing that he didn't lock it, "Yeah, bout 5 to 10 minutes tops."

Travis smiled and shook his head. Just as she suspected, he knew she was lying. He placed his pistol on the end table, "So, why did my girl Malaysia say that Lacy was gone for 3 hours? She had been following her the entire time. And the moment Lacy left the room, she called Kesha and told her, and Kesha told you to go over there. According to Kesha, you went right to his room, and you were in there for 2 hours, until she walked out the room and knocked on the door, trying to get you to hurry up. Then she had to rush back to her room, so he wouldn't see her. She was giving you the signal to hurry up. So, you tell me that you were only there for 10 minutes, tops?" he paused, "And plus, that's the fuckin' Peabody Hotel. The most expensive hotel in the city. They got cameras everywhere, on every floor. My girl at the front desk reviewed the tape and said you went in the room at 8:15 and came out at 10:30. That's when Lacy got off the elevator and ran into you."

Kita thought about what he just said to her. She knew she was fucked. She needed someone to help save her ass because she knew Travis was going to kill her. Again, she looked at the front door. She wanted to make sure that she wasn't tripping and that it was unlocked.

Travis noticed the sweat dripping off her forehead, "So, I ask you again. Why is he still alive? Why didn't you kill him that night?" he leaned forward on the couch.

"Trap," she cried, "I...I...I... think he put a few perc 30s in my drink. I must have passed out. When I woke up, I heard the shower running, and I was naked. He told me to hurry up and get out. I wasn't in my right mind then. I was moving slow. But, I'm on top of my shit now. I haven't had any in a few days. Please, Trap," at that moment, Travis' door swung open. Two men stood there with their guns drawn.

"Don't even think about it, Trap," the young guys said, as he noticed Travis getting ready to reach for his pistol. Kita quickly stood to her feet and looked at Travis smiling.

"What took you nigga's so fuckin' long? This nigga damn near choked the life out of me," she walked over to Travis and slapped him in his face twice, "That's for choking me and thinking I was gonna turn on Dawg for your petty ass. Nigga fuck you! I told you I was on my shit now!" she spit in his face, "And that's for having my cousin Big Marvin killed," she smiled as she walked behind the two gunmen. She continued to spill the beans, "See, Dawg knew that you sent me. And he promised that if I would turn the tables on you that he would give me 50 bands, which ya' sorry ass didn't offer! So, I got high, got fucked, and got 10 bands up front," she laughed as one of the gunmen took Travis' gun off the table, and the other one made him stand up. Travis smiled. He didn't care about dying. He shook his head at Dawg's sloppy plan and started clapping.

"Nigga, you about to die, and you up here clapping?" one of the gunmen said.

Kita was tired of all the preliminaries, "I'ma tell y'all like Dawg told me. Nigga just be like Nike, Just Do It! Fuck all this talkin'!" she screamed.

Travis stopped clapping, but continued smiling, "I see you two dumb fucks never watch Power. I'm Ghost and Dawg is Tommy. I always win," at that moment, Kesha came out the back blasting, hitting one of the gunmen in the chest as the other one turned to her. Travis reached in the back of his waist and pulled out another glock and unloaded his clip on the other one. Overkill. Kita turned to run out, but was stopped by Tameka. She instantly pissed on herself because she knew she was about to meet her demise.

"Wait, Trap!" Kita cried, "Please don't kill me," she got on her knees pleading for her life.

"Bitch, get the fuck up," Travis slapped her with the back of his hand twice, "That's for puttin' yo' hands on me. You know betta' than that! And I can't believe you turned on me. After I saved your brother's life in the pen," he spit in Kita's face and hit her with his fist, "And that's for spittin' on me, you "pill junkie"!" he paused and smirked, "But, I ain't completely heartless. I'm not gon' kill you. Besides, I'm hungry," he turned and walked back to the kitchen.

Kita looked at Kesha holding a gun to her head. She knew that Kesha wasn't going to hurt her because they had been friends since the 3rd grade, and they had been eating each other's pussy since 12th grade. She felt safe.

"Kesha, you know I'm sprung on them damn pills. I'm sick."

"I know babe, I'ma get you some help," Kesha said, as tears formed in her eyes. She lowered her gun and Kita's breathing slowed down almost to its normal pace, as she wiped her eyes, "You gon' get some help today," Kesha turned and sat on the couch.

Kita stood by the door shaking, "Thank you, Keesh. You know what's best for me. I do need some help. Help me, Keesh."

"Okay. Calm down, calm down. Your help is here."

Pow! Pow! Pow!

Tameka put three holes in the back of Kita's skull. She stood over the body watching the blood pool around her head until Travis walked back into the room. He was eating a bag of plain Lays potato chips and nodding his head in approval.

"Job well done!" he complimented.

She looked up at him, "Trap, my debt is paid," she was a known killer, and she knew, although Travis gave her a pass at the funeral, that didn't mean he wouldn't kill her then, especially if she gave him another reason to. She looked him directly in his eyes. Tameka held on to her pistol extremely tight with her finger still on the trigger, "Trap, I'm sorry about pulling a gun on you at the funeral. But I didn't want you two to kill each other, and I still don't want that," Tameka paused, "But you know my daughter, Teeuni and her husband Guy, moved to Cashville, and they just had my grandchild," the word "child" hit home with Travis. He was a new father, so he sympathized with her, "I'm a grandmother now, so Trap, I'm out of the game. Yo' sista' was right about what she said at Dre's funeral," Tameka dropped her head in shame, "I did leave her in the Jungle the day she was raped. I hated Lacy's stuck up ass. Mane, she used to laugh at me when Nell made a fool outta me. I hate Nell ass too, but I wasn't crazy enough to touch Nell though...that woulda been a suicide mission," she laughed, "And, to be honest, I watched the whole rape from the other end of the Jungle. Shit, I was smokin' a blunt while Lacy was screamin'. See...I been a heartless bitch for a long time. Hyde Park made me like that, but I can't do this shit no more. Trap, I'm leaving town right now. I don't want to see Dawg or you ever again," she walked up to him and kissed him on the check, "We good, Trap?"

"We good. But if I see you around here again, before Dawg is dead, I'ma kill you."

"I wish you two could be brothers again, but I'm out. Love you guys," Tameka slowly backed out of the house. She wanted no more drama with the two "frenemies". She wanted to be there for her grandchild, and she was determined that her crime-filled past was not about to steal what she knew would be the best part of her life.

Kesha looked at Travis and the three bodies sprawled out on the floor. She smiled and shook her head, as she reached in her pocket and grabbed her cellphone.

"Hey, who you callin'?" Travis eyed Kesha suspiciously.

"Look at yo' floor mane. You already know what I'm doin'. I'm callin' our people to clean this mess up," she said in an aggravated tone.

"Bitch, don't get no fuckin' attitude! Do what you do...but don't pull that shit you pulled with T.T.'s body. That shit was messy, and I'm still upset about that. Just make sure these bodies don't end up on the gotdamn news this time! I want these muthafucka's to be ashes before night falls," Travis ordered calmly.

Kesha rolled her eyes and blew out a frustrated breath, "Mane look, I don' told you a thousand times that Dre' told me YOU wanted me to leave T.T. body in that van in Hyde Park. You keep blamin'..."

Travis threw his hand up for her to stop talking, "I don't got time for that right now Keesh. It don't matter anyway," he glanced at the picture of Luther at his college graduation. He remembered proudly hanging it on the wall next to his grandmother's picture years before, "Dre' is dead, and so is that excuse. Anyway, thanks for staying at the house for me. I knew somebody was gon' try me here. Dawg knew I'd never leave my granny house. And he played his hand. Good move," he stared at the bodies, "It just wasn't good enough. That trap ended wrong, this war is getting ready to end too.

Chapter 9

NOT MY BABY

Ring... Ring… Ring...

Travis was sitting in his granny's house with Kesha, and his cell phone started ringing back to back. He ignored it at first because he was coming up with new strategies to get at Dawg however, the ringing continued.

"Hello," he answered without looking at the name on the screen. It was Malaysia.

"Traaap," she cried, "Something is wrong with Laura-Anne!!! I just got here to Lebonheur Children's Hospital downtown about 5 minutes ago, and they just took her to the back. She ain't doin' good," she screamed into the phone.

Travis hung up the phone and told Kesha they had to get to the hospital ASAP. They jumped up and raced to his car. Before the doors were even closed, he was burning rubber out of the driveway. They sped down Chelsea Ave. until they made a quick left on Dunlap St. Travis was speeding, mad, and beating on his dashboard.

"What the fuck happened to my baby?" he shouted out loud to no one in particular. For the first time in years, Kesha saw tears roll down Travis' face. She rocked back and forth on the passenger side as he ran through every light on Dunlap. Kesha knew if Laura-Anne were to die, so would her best friend. She knew ever since the baby was born that he wanted a new life. But the devil kept coming at him. Travis was determined to beat all odds. He simply wanted to live in peace, but he was obviously in the middle of his "reaping season" because he had sown so many evil seeds that his life was on the line daily. The devil wanted to break him down like a double barrel shotgun. But for some reason, God was still fighting for him to win. At least that's what Kesha assumed.

They turned into the parking lot, parked, and ran through the emergency entrance. When they made it to the desk, Kesha did all the talking. Travis was struggling with his emotions and couldn't talk.

"Laura-Anne Stewart, was brought in here about 10 minutes ago," Kesha informed the young woman at the receptionist's desk while trying to catch her breath.

"And you are?" the receptionist asked.

"This is the child's father," Kesha pointed to Travis, and motioned for him to show the young woman his ID.

The receptionist looked at the ID approvingly, and then typed in the name "Stewart", she scrolled down the screen until she saw Laura-Anne's name and clicked on it.

"Oh yeah, I remember them rushing her in. She's in the ICU. Go straight down that hallway," she pointed, "And make a right. There, you will see an arrow on the wall that says ICU. You probably won't be able to go in right now, but her mother; Malaysia Garrison, is in the room across from it."

"That ain't her fuckin' mama," Kesha nastily informed the woman, and ran to catch up with Travis because he had taken off running before the receptionist finished giving directions. They jetted down the hallway and made it to the ICU in record time. When they walked into the area, they looked over in the waiting room and spotted Malaysia walking around in circles, talking to herself, and biting her nails.

Travis busted into the room, "Lay Lay, what the fuck happened? Where's my baby? Is she gon' be ok?" Travis anxiously waited on a response, but Malaysia was an emotional wreck. She was shaking like the last leaf on the tree as the wind blew one hundred miles per hour. She was about to fall, "Come on Laysia. Sit down," Travis tried to get her to relax, so he could find out what he needed to know. He wrapped his arms around her as she cried uncontrollable tears of sorrow and pain, "She's gon' be alright. I know she is," Travis said, although he didn't know what was actually wrong with his baby, "Keesh, go find me a doctor or somebody to tell me what's going on."

Kesha rushed out the room to find someone who could tell Travis something about his baby. He nervously thought about the possibility of losing his daughter, and he knew he wouldn't be able to take it. Along with everything else he had lost in his life; he was slowly losing his grip on sanity altogether. Travis looked down at the diary Malaysia was holding, as she rocked in his arms.

"Lay Lay, please tell me what happened. How did y'all end up here?"

However, before she could answer him, Kesha came back into the room with the doctor. Travis instantly stood to his feet.

"Hi, Mr. Stewart," the female doctor said as she smiled at him in pity because she knew he had seen the inside of a hospital several times over the last few years. She had been their family doctor ever since the Stewart boys came into money.

"Of course, you know I'm Dr. Morris. I just started working here about a month ago," she said with a warm, concerned smile.

"I know, Doc," Travis said, panicking and nervous, "How is my baby?" She took a deep breath as her shoulders went up, "To be truthful, Laura-Anne has what we medical professionals call: 'Shaken Baby Syndrome'."

"What the fuck?" Travis yelled, as his eyes shifted to Malaysia. She was the last person with his baby, and when he left his daughter she was just fine. Anger and rage entered his mind and heart, as he moved closer to Malaysia. She backed away, still remaining silent, "What the fuck happened?" Travis asked Malaysia, but Dr. Morris answered.

"Mr. Stewart, there are a number of things that could have caused this. But the main thing that we need to be praying for is that this does not destroy your child's brain cells. And that it does not prevent her brain from getting enough oxygen. If that happens, she will be brain dead. Unfortunately, that's all I can tell you at this moment. We are working diligently on her now. I must get back to her. I'll be back as soon as I have some good news for you. For now, I need you all to stay strong and pray," Dr. Morris left the waiting room and headed back into surgery.

Travis turned to Malaysia and asked for the last time. He gripped her by the arm and looked back at Kesha. She walked over to the door and secured it. She knew that Travis didn't give a fuck about killing Malaysia right where she stood if she didn't start talking.

Through gritted teeth, Travis asked, "For the last time, what the fuck happened to my baby, your fuckin' niece?" Malaysia was crestfallen as she cried and tried to explain at the same time.

"I walked out of the... and… and… when I walked back in, she was choking," she paused, and tried to pull away from Travis' death grip. She also watched the entrance to the waiting room. "I...I...I... picked her up and patted her on the back and then," she shook her head from side to side, "But she wouldn't stop choking. I patted her a little harder, I guess after she didn't stop, I panicked and shook her just a little, and she coughed. So I thought she was ok," she sat back down, "So when we walked into the kitchen, I was getting ready to feed her a bottle, but I noticed that she wouldn't eat, and she started breathing funny. So, I dialed 911. And before they arrived, she vomited," tears streamed down her face, "I didn't know what to do. Trap, I tried all I knew. I didn't want to bother you until I came here. I knew you had a lot going on."

He placed his arms around her and whispered in her ear that everything was going to be ok. She saw Kesha walk away from the door and take her seat. Malaysia knew at that moment, she had gotten away with murder... well... attempted murder, and an evil smirk appeared on her face. She knew she had lied to Travis. The truth was that she wanted to be the one that gave him his first child, and she knew that that chance was over. Unless, she somehow got rid of Laura-Anne. However, she knew if the doctor came back and told him anything different to contradict what she said, that she was a dead woman walking. Her only solution was to get to the doctor before Travis did. She whispered in his ear.

"Baby, go home and handle that business with Dawg, so we can get out of this city. I'll stay with our daughter."

"Fuck that! I ain't goin' nowhere until they tell me my gotdamn daughter is gon' be alright. I pray they don't come back and tell me nothin' different," he lifted Malaysia's chin and gazed into her hypnotic gray eyes,

"Baby, please, for your sake, let your story be true. Because if it's not, I promise you, I'ma send yo' pretty ass on the first train smokin' straight to wherever ya' psychotic ass sister, and my brother ended up! At least my brother will be happy then...that nigga will finally have you!" Travis got up and paced the room for a few seconds, before saying he would be right back. Kesha sat in silence glaring at Malaysia.

Malaysia ignored Kesha's obvious hatred of her, the feeling was mutual.

Slowly, she opened her diary, closed her eyes, and thought of what she wanted to write:

Love is like two people on a seesaw, when one goes up the other one goes down. The balance between the two of them is always fucked. Because the one that's up doesn't want to be up, and the one that's down doesn't want to be down. However, the pain is there in both cases. I only know one way to get rid of pain, and that is to give a little back. I know it's immature, but that's the pain I felt. (I was wrong. Dead wrong!) I love this man, but the pain he caused me years ago, still hurts.

Although he is really trying to make it right. I'm fucked up because I can't let it go and be patient. The anguish my sister caused me, still hurts. But how was she supposed to know I loved him. We were all Tangled In A Lover's Web. I fucked up. I took it out on the wrong person. An innocent baby. I love my niece; his daughter, but I never meant to hurt her, I just wanted her gone. That's why I intentionally shook her, but I didn't mean to cause her the pain I did. I love her too. Crazy love makes you do childish and immature shit. Now I know I'm truly fucked up. Lord, I asked you to forgive me for what I was about to do. And I know you did. But, please don't let her be brain dead. Please Lord! I'm just as fucked up as my crazy ass sister Victoria was. I guess we got that from our daddy side. Love... Damn! Why does it have to cause pain? Why does it cause our minds to react stupidly? Crazy Love... Somehow, Lord, you gots to fix this situation, and while you're at it...fix MY crazy ass, Trap's vengeful ass, Lacy's confused ass, and Dawg's stupid ass...FIX IT! Oh...and God...please give me the strength not to beat this bitch Kesha's ass up in this waiting room. She keeps starin' at me, so she obviously thinks my fine ass won't tear this muthafucka' up. Amen.

Chapter 10

LAST TRY

Word traveled through Hyde Park that Travis' daughter was in critical condition at LeBonheur Hospital, and she needed everyone's prayers. Dawg's heart was broken for his best friend, brother, and family. Despite their beef, Laura-Anne was still his niece. He decided that if the beef was going to end, the time had come.

Dawg got up and called Lacy to inform her of her niece's situation, and that he was going to try to reach out to him at the hospital. He knew Travis wouldn't try to kill him on camera, in broad daylight. He was too smart for that.

When she picked up the phone, he gave her the sad news, and she screamed in his ear, "I'm a few minutes from your house. Wait for me! Babe. This is wayyy out of control! My brother so pissed at me, he didn't even call to tell me about the baby! This shit has got to end! I'm tired!" she screamed, "Oh God! Poor Laura-Anne."

"Aight, come on. I'll be waiting in the car," Dawg ran through the house checking everything. He set the alarm, grabbed his keys, and walked out. By the time he started the car, Lacy pulled into the driveway. She hopped in his car, and they sped off.

The two of them pulled into the parking lot and spotted Travis' blue Cutlass. They looked at each other nervously. Dawg cocked his 45 and put it in his waist.

"What the fuck you need that for?" asked Lacy.

"We tryna' bring peace, but sometimes, bruh can be a real hot head, so," he shrugged his shoulders, as he got out of the car, "I'ma be safe too," he glanced at her purse, "So, you telling me that you don't have that lil 32 I gave you in there?" he patted her purse and got out.

"Yeah, but I have never taken it out. You told me to keep it there, so that's what I did," she tried to explain, "I have done everything you told me to do," Lacy's phone rang loudly and interrupted their conversation. She quickly answered it, "Hello," she listened, "Oh, Erica. I'm sorry I had to leave for an emergency. I'll call you when I'm on my way back. Thanks for understanding," Lacy had forgotten that she asked Erica to come over and help her clean up her new house.

When they arrived at the hospital, they walked through the main entrance and went to the desk. Lacy gave the receptionist Laura-Anne's name.

"You look just like her, she got to be your relative," the receptionist smiled and waved away the ID that Lacy was trying to show her, "I don't need to see that, you are most definitely that baby's family. She is a hazel-eyed doll. Everyone that was here when she came in instantly fell in love with her. We're all praying that she pulls through, she's so young."

At that moment, Travis walked into the lobby. His eyes locked with Lacy's, then with Dawg's. He slowly eased his shirt up and reached for his pistol. He then thought about the hospital cameras and cut his eyes at the security guard near the door. Smartly, he pulled his shirt back down and decided to handle the situation differently.

"Naw, that bitch ain't my daughter's relative. She ain't no kin to us!" he told the receptionist while staring at Dawg. He noticed the bulge in Dawg's waist. He knew he had a gun. Dawg stared sadly at his old friend and remained silent. He raised his hands in surrender. He was frustrated with Travis because he was still trying to get revenge for Luther, when his only child's life was hanging by a very thin thread. Dawg knew that the children's hospital was not the place for their foolishness, and he knew deep down that Travis knew it too.

"Trap, I come in peace. I just came to check on your baby," Dawg said solemnly.

"Fuck you," he mumbled, walking up on Dawg, "She's gon' be alright."

Lacy could see that her twin's body was tense, and that he was worried.

"Y'all get a pass today. Get the fuck out of here!" he looked at Lacy, "And bitch, I think you brought this nigga here to kill me. Y'all thought y'all was gon' catch me slippin'," Travis eased his pistol out of his waist and pulled it around to the front under his shirt. The receptionist looked oddly at everyone. She could tell that Travis and Lacy were sister and brother. However, she was a street-smart woman, so she looked away. Eventually, she got up and walked off. She wasn't a nosy woman, so she wanted no parts of what she thought was about to transpire.

Lacy started crying at the way her brother spoke to her, "Travis, how could you think I would bring…"

He cut her off, "Bitch, save them tears. You act as if you don't see that nigga with that pistol on him. Hoe, you crazy as fuck. You ain't a Stewart, you whatever your adopted parents said you was. Our sorry ass daddy did right to sell you, like you just sold me... out!"

"Trap, that's ya' sister! But since that don't mean shit to you. That's STILL my fuckin' woman, and she ain't gon' be no mo' bitches," Dawg chimed in.

Finally, they were about to face off. The time had come in the most unlikely place, "Fuck you nigga, this shit ain't got to go no further. Let's do this," Lacy cried, as two police officers entered the hospital through the ER doors. They were escorting a social worker that was holding a screaming toddler in her arms. The child appeared to have been beaten up. While the social worker was filling out the proper paperwork, the officers saw Dawg and Travis face-to-face, looking like they were about to start some serious trouble. One of the officers was the rookie that came with Captain Reid to Travis' house a few days before.

Travis eased his pistol back down into his briefs as the two officers approached them.

"If it ain't 'Mr. Un-fuckin' Touchable' Travis Stewart," his eyes shifted to Dawg, "And I'm assuming you're the one he's out to kill. Keith aka Dawg. Do you bark?" he laughed. He took out his cellphone and called Captain Reid. He told the other officer to keep his eye on Dawg as he stood next to Travis. When the Captain answered, he went right into snitch mode, "Captain, I got your boy Travis and the other guy; Dawg, face to face at LeBonheur Hospital. From the looks of it, they were about to kill each other," he listened, "Yes, Sir. Will do. Place your hand on the counter for us please," Dawg did as he was asked, but Travis looked at the rookie as if he were crazy.

"You don't have probable cause to come in here and harass us."

Dawg thought about what Travis told the officer, and he knew he was right. He immediately turned around, crossed his arms, and smiled at the other officer who was about to search him. Travis shook his head in disgust at Dawg. He knew better, "Get ya' ass back on the phone with my boy Captain Reid and tell him that Trap said to come search me his gotdamn self. I'm out of here," Travis knew if he allowed them to search him, they would find his pistol, and he would be facing another felony charge. The courts would then career him out as a three-time felon, and he wouldn't see his daughter until she turned 21. He walked to the exit door and rushed to his car. Dawg and Lacy wasted no time following suit.

Travis made it to his car and slowly drove past Lacy and Dawg with his pistol in his lap. He wanted to bust but saw the two officers standing by the door staring at him. Instead, he yelled out, "It ain't over yet, but we close to the end. One of us is goin' to see our maker; *'The Devil or God'*, within the next 48 hours," he sped off into traffic and called Kesha.

"Hey Keesh. Some shit happened in the lobby. Dawg had the nerve to show up," he explained, "The police came in, so I left. Catch an Uber to my crib. I'll pay for it," he listened, "Thanks love."

Lacy couldn't control herself any longer. Her body went limp right before they made it to the car, and she almost passed out. Dawg picked her up and placed her gently in his car, "I knew you shouldn't have come. Now, not only does he hate you, but now he doesn't care if he kills me in the process of getting to you," she whispered, "Dawg, I love you, but this ain't gon' work," she cried softly, "He's the only real family I have. I don't want to lose him," she leaned over and kissed him on the cheek, "Nor you baby. It's best that I remove myself from the picture for now. And I pray that you leave town today," she took a deep breath. Her love for him was genuine and pure, "And if you do, let me know. I'll go with you."

Dawg was speechless. He thought about everything he had accomplished and everything he was going to leave behind if he ran like a coward. He feared no man, but he knew that Travis wasn't going to let it go. It was either kill or be killed.

"Give me 48 hours to get all my shit in order, sell a couple of cars right quick, get my aunt Jackie to oversee my businesses so my money will continue to flow, and we out this bitch. I promise," he pleaded as he held her hand. She slowly pulled away.

"Okay, 48 hours. If you ain't ready to go by then, I'ma move on," she took a deep breath and got out of the car. She wanted to be alone, so she started walking off.

"Lacy, where you going? Remember, you rode up here with me," asked Dawg, as he threw his hands up in the air.

"I'ma call me an Uber. I need to clear my head without you," she turned and continued to walk away, "48 Hours Dawg!" she yelled back.

Lacy pulled out her phone and called Erica, "Hey, sister in law, can you come get me from Lebonheur please," she listened to Erica panicking, "Oh, I don't really know how Laura-Anne is doing, but I will fill you in on everything once you get here, and can you please take me to my crib downtown," again she listened, "Ok, say less, see you in a bit."

Chapter 11

CHANGE OF PLANS

Dawg did as he promised and made all the necessary arrangements for him and Lacy to leave town. He felt in his heart that it was time to move on. He had outgrown the city of Memphis; well at least North Memphis.

He called his aunt to give her instructions.

"Aunt Jackie, I need you to know that if anything happens to me, I want you to call this number. 201.8860, and simply say, 'he's gone'. And tell them what happened. I'ma bring you an envelope to give to them."

"Baby, you gon' be just fine. Stop talking like that. If ya' mama was alive…!" aunt Jackie shouted.

"You ain't gotta say it…I know my mama woulda' been actin' a fool about me leavin' Memphis in the first place. I'm just sayin'. Just in case somethin' happens…. But this is what I'ma need for you to do. Please... promise me that you will do it."

"I promise, Keith. But I don't like the sound of your voice. But okay. Goodbye. I can't stand this kind of talkin'. You and that damn Travis boy always into somethin'. Now y'all at each other's throats! If something happens to you, I'ma call the police and tell them he did it. Fuck this shit, I ain't gon' sit around here and let somethin' happen to you and don't call the police. Since yo' mama gone, and Rick gone, you all I got! Hell, this mess you and that boy got goin' on got my son killed. Rick was my ONLY child! I'm gotdamn 73 years old, I ain't got time for no more of this bullshit! Enough is enough!" she yelled, and Dawg listened, "I don't wanna hear no more about this mess right now! Get ya' ass off my phone. And I love you!"

"I love you too auntie," Dawg said, although his aunt Jackie had already hung up. He made one more call.

"Aye, I talked to my aunt," he listened, "Yeah, Jackie. She crazy as hell, but I gave her the rundown. So, she knows what to do. Take care, and I'll holla atcha' later. Me and Lacy about moving up out this bitch. So, I'll hit you up. Peace. 100."

Trap's Granny's House

"Okay, listen up everybody. I got somethin' goin'. I'm just waitin' on my people on the inside to get at me on his whereabouts. And when that happens, I need for everybody to be on 'go mode'."

Travis looked around the room and noticed that one man was staring out the window, "Old man, are you payin' attention? Because this shit needs to be flawless! I got the Captain breathin' up my ass, and my daughter in the hospital fighting for her gotdamn life! So, I need you to pay attention!" he shouted. The old man shook his head in agreeance, but he was tired of Travis telling him what to do, however, he really wanted to help him end the madness.

"What if shit goes South? Do we stick to the plan, or just make sure everyone is dead?" The old man asked.

"Just do your part and it will fall in place," Travis assured him.

"Okay, Boss," the old man said, sarcastically and started back glaring out the window. This time, what he was looking at looked back. That's when his suspicion manifested, "Well, Boss, they're out there. I was watching this black Crown Vic for twenty minutes, and now I know it's the police," Travis and a few more of his henchmen rushed to the window, "They've been sitting out there for at least 30 minutes watching this house and taking pictures of everybody's car," he looked at Travis and smiled, "I'm sure they ran everybody's tags by now," he walked away from the window and took a seat, "We need to erase them as well."

"Change of plans," Travis said, as he reached in his pocket and pulled out his phone. He continued to stand in the window, as everyone moved about.

He listened to the phone ring on the other end, and when they picked up, he got straight down to business, "Okay, I'll give you the 50 bands cash that you asked for. Now the ball in ya' court. Make it happen," he listened, "Bet, say less," he turned to his crew, "Okay, it's gotta happen tonight. I'm just waiting on one more phone call. And I'll tell y'all where it's going down from that point. So be ready. I'm about to go back to the hospital to check on my daughter."

The old man chimed in, "Boss, you need me to go with you. You know, to watch your back."

"Thanks, but Kesha goin' with me. I trust her more than anybody in this room. It's not about a check with her. It's all about loyalty."

Lebonheur Children's Hospital

Travis and Kesha walked back into the hospital and headed straight for room 212. Malaysia called him with the good news. The baby was going to be just fine. That was the best news he had heard in the last few days. They rushed into the room and saw Malaysia rocking the baby with tears in her eyes.

"What's wrong, Lay Lay?" he asked out of concern, "You said the doctor said Laura-Anne was going to be just fine. So, why you crying?" he sat beside her, wrapped his arms around her, and kissed her cheeks. Kesha watched from afar. She knew something was a little off with the scene. However, she didn't say anything to Travis. He had too much on his plate.

"Yeah, I'm just glad she's going to be alright. I was so scared," Malaysia admitted.

"By the way, what did the doctor say?" Travis took the baby out of Malaysia's arms.

Nervously, she said, "Next time, try not to shake her so hard. And hold her facing down," Kesha coughed at the same time saying… *'bullshit'*. Travis didn't catch it, but Malaysia did. However, she chose not to address it at the moment. She knew she had to keep Travis calm.

"That's it? Wow, I thought it would be more to it. I need to talk to her."

"No! I mean, that's what you left me in charge for. IF I'm going to be her stepmom one day, you gotta let me handle some things, baby," she kissed him as her eyes stayed focused on Kesha. She knew that Kesha had to go, because if not, she might find out the truth, and Travis would kill her for what she tried to do to his daughter.

"I guess you're right," he hugged his baby and breathed in her sweet-smelling, innocent scent, "Daddy, loves you sweetheart. I promise I'ma take good care of you."

Malaysia stood and walked into the restroom. Kesha seized the opportunity. She wanted to find out what was going on with Malaysia. They never had any real problems that she was aware of, other than the incident where Kesha was caught giving Travis head. Malaysia never forgot about that day because that one incident led to Luther seducing her to get back at Travis. His plan of revenge turned into a tangled "web" of deceit that lasted over a decade.

Kesha eased over to the windowsill where Malaysia left her diary and started talking to the baby. Discreetly, she eased the diary into the waist of her jeans. Travis was too focused on his daughter to pay Kesha any attention. All he wanted to do was get her out of the hospital and back home safely with him.

"Trap, I'll be in the hallway. I gotta make sure Dawg don't show back up," Kesha stepped out in the hallway and thumbed through the diary until she stumbled across the part where she saw the word "shake". As she quickly read it, her eyes popped open when she realized that Malaysia had shaken the baby on purpose. She was trying to kill the three-month-old. In the diary, she also explained that Laura-Anne had to die because she wanted to give Travis his first child, "Dirty bitch! Trap won't be marrying this bitch because I'ma kill her. ASAP," Kesha took out her phone. As she tried to decide the best way to handle the situation, she turned around and came face-to-face with Malaysia.

"So, you read my diary?" she snatched it out of her hand and stepped closer to Kesha. Malaysia truly didn't want any problems with Kesha. She was well aware of her skills, but her love for Travis would have made her stand up against King Kong, "Listen, I'm not about to let you destroy my lil family. Kesha, I fucked up," she whispered, looking back at the door to Laura-Anne's room, "but I promise it won't happen again."

"You damn right it won't," *Smack!* Kesha hit Malaysia in her face so hard with the back of her hand that she left a hand print on her face, "Because I'ma break both of your hands. Then I'ma tell Trap, and he's gon' kill you himself."

Malaysia grabbed her face and stumbled into the door to Laura-Anne's hospital room. She quickly stabilized her balance and threw her hands up to fight, but she spoke in a low tone. She didn't want Travis to hear.

"Wait, Kesha, "You know I got plenty of money, and you know what Travis is going through. Please! I'm begging you not to say shit," they circled each other in fight mode, "I love Trap, Kesha. I'll give you 200 bands not to say nothing. I promise I will never do anything to that baby ever, again. You have my word," Kesha thought about all that she could do with the money, but her loyalty was with Travis.

"Bitch," Kesha said, looking back at the door, hoping Travis wouldn't walk out, "I want 400. And that's non-negotiable."

"Deal."

Kesha walked back into the room as Travis got up off the bed. She saw how sad he looked and shook her head. She then looked over at Malaysia, "I can't do it bitch! You was wrong!" she then turned to Travis.

"Fam. Listen, we really need to talk and fast."

"Not now, Keesh. It's about my baby right now," Travis dismissed her.

"But, Trap. It's important."

"I said, NOT NOW! Damn! Kesha, is you harda hearin'? We already in the hospital, go get that shit checked out or somethin', but get the fuck outta here if you can't respect what I just said," Travis cut his eyes at Kesha to let her know he was not playing with her.

"Aight, we'll talk later," Kesha left the room and Malaysia smirked at her as she left.

Lacy's House

Lacy and Erica sat around the house sipping wine as Lacy explained to her about what transpired at the hospital. She was torn. She couldn't believe her twin brother would talk to her as though she were not his sister.

"So, you see, Erica. I'm stuck between a rock and a hard place. I love my brother. He has been my guardian angel all my life," she took a deep breath, "But on the other hand, I can't fuck him, and he can't give me the love and attention only a man than loves his woman can give me back. That's where Dawg comes in. He's a real cool guy. He treats me well, and the dick is off the chain. Bitch, when I tell you that nigga puts it down, he puts it down. And let's not talk about how long his tongue is. Hoe, he will eat this pussy until I say stop. Actually, he won't stop when I say stop because he loves to drive me up a wall. He be havin' me screamin' his name for real," laughed Lacy, as she crossed her legs from the thought of making love to Dawg, "See, I wish they could just go back to being friends."

Erica listened, but she wasn't feeling the conversation. She hated Dawg because he played a role in Luther's death. However, despite the tragedy, she was still going to be rolling in the money for a long time. Her baby's last name was going to be Stewart.

"But, Lacy. You have to understand how Travis feels. That was his baby brother. He took care of him when they had nothing."

"But that lil muthafucka saw me get raped in the jungle and did nothing. On top of that, he has taunted me ever since. When me and Vicki used to hang out, he would call me all types of fucked up names, and he was always tryna' make her not be my friend. It seemed like he wanted to make me miserable," she said, angrily. Lacy was at the end of her abyss and struggling to balance herself from falling into forever. She needed to get away. She could only pray that Dawg would hurry up and take her away from all the madness that had spiraled out of control. However, she never let on to Erica that she was about to break down. She did her best to stay strong.

"Yeah, I've heard, but he was 11, Lacy. And look at you now. Successful and happy. And not to mention, he was your brother too," she softened her tone, "That boy loved you too. So, think about losing a real family member," she paused for effect, "Don't lose your only real brother for some good dick. That shit comes and goes."

Lacy stood and looked around the house, "You might be right. This was his house. Travis gave it to me," Erica was shocked to hear that part. She had never been in his house. An opportunist thought came to mind.

"Let me show you around. The view from the balcony of the master suite is the dopest shit you'll ever see. You can stare right out at the "M" Bridge and into the Mississippi River," Lacy offered a tour, but the doorbell rang.

She looked at her Ring app, and saw Dawg standing on the other side of the door, "It's my baby. Go on and look around. Make yourself at home."

"Oh, I'm at home because this is gon' be my house real soon," Erica mumbled. She walked through the house talking to herself, "My picture would look good in here, and this will be the baby's room, and this will be my 'Woman Cave'. Yes, I will be a Stewart," Erica heard Dawg's voice and thought that it was time for her to go. She didn't want to be the third wheel, "Lacy, I'ma go ahead and leave."

"You don't have to go. Give me a few minutes."

Erica walked upstairs to find the master suite that Lacy was bragging about. When she got there, she walked out on the balcony and was blown away by the view, "Damnnn! Lacy was right! This shit is breathtaking!" she breathed in the fresh air and sent a text. She could see herself out there on a cool fall night, leaning on the rail letting some man hit her from the back, "Yes, this is going to be home for me and my son one day soon," she rubbed her swollen baby.

****The Call****

While Travis was waiting on Laura-Anne to be discharged, his phone rang. He looked down at it but did not answer. He looked at Kesha and said, "Okay, what is it? What was you so pressed to tell me earlier?"

The baby started crying and halted Kesha's story because Travis blew her off again to attend to his child.

Malaysia walked up to Kesha and said, "500 bands. Please don't do it. Please," she whispered to her. At that very moment, Travis looked down at his phone and saw the code and address he had been waiting on.

"Malaysia, take the baby!" he said hurriedly, "Kesha, let's go! It's on now. You got your pistols?" she raised her shirt up, "Ok, you can tell me wassup in the car."

Kesha looked at Malaysia, then at Travis, "Come on, it wasn't shit. Let's ride."

Travis led the way out of the hospital room and Kesha slow-dragged on purpose. She watched Travis walking ahead of her and leaned over to whisper to Malaysia.

"I want a whole fuckin' million bitch! I know you got it! You out here ridin' in a $300,000 car and shit! Errbody know that Korean mufucka' you was married to was worth over a billion. And...to be honest, I don't even know if I'm even gon' take the money. I'm still thinkin' about it. So... just get with yo' bank or do whateva' you gotta do while we gone to pull the million together. IF I decide to take it, I will let you know when we get back. If I don't decide to take it, that means you gon' have to face Trap, and you already know how that's gon' turn out," Kesha smiled and started walking towards the door.

"Kesha, I don't like it when people do me like that. Tell me now. I ain't gon' be able to think straight not knowing whether Trap knows or not. Come on mane," Malaysia begged.

Kesha stopped, "Bitch please! Now you know how Trap felt not knowing if his daughter was gon' live or not. I ain't finna make you comfortable hoe. Deal with that shit! You tried to hurt that lil baby for what? Cuz you wanted to be his first baby mama?" she shook her head,

"You so fuckin' stupid, he ain't got no son, yo' dumb ass coulda' gave him that. You still woulda' gave him a first!" she smirked at Malaysia, "Shit, maybe when he kills yo' ignant ass, I'll give him a son," she rubbed her empty stomach, "Yeah hoe! Fuck you! Like I said, you'll get my answer when you get it," she shook her head at Malaysia and ran to catch up with Travis.

Chapter 12

IT'S ABOUT TO GO DOWN

The sun had set, and the timing was right. Travis called his entire crew to his house to give the final instructions. He made a few more calls to ensure everyone's safety. As they arrived at his house, he drove around the block a couple of times to make sure that no cops were watching his place.

"Cool, the coast is clear," he pulled into his garage and immediately closed the door. Everyone came prepared to complete the mission. Kesha, however, seemed to be focused on something else. Her mind wasn't on the mission and Travis noticed, "Keesh, come on, get ya' head in the game. This ain't no damn rehearsal! I need you on point!"

Kesha had finally had enough of Travis snapping on her, "Look, nigga. You keep snappin' on the one person that's gon' ride with you to the end, and you over here bein' extra nice to these fake ass people. If you feel you gots to talk to me like I'm one of the niggas that you give orders to, then I can walk the fuck on!" Kesha stressed, as she was about to hit the garage door button to exit.

"What the fuck you talkin' bout, Keesh?" asked Travis.

"Look mane. Mo3 and Boosie said it best, 'Errbody ain't ya' partner, Errbody ain't ya friend.' I'm saying that because I've never crossed you and always been 100 with you. Look around. Everybody that's pulling up, doin' this hit cuz it's their job, but me; I'm not gettin' shit out of this! I'm doing it because I love you!"

"Love me?" Travis looked at her strangely, "As in..."

"Never mind. Let's get this shit done. But when it's over, I'm out,"

Kesha decided to take the mill from Malaysia and leave while she still could. She knew Travis loved that evil bitch, so she had to let him find out the hard way.

Travis was at a loss for words. Losing someone that he really loved fucked his head up. He knew the feeling too well. He exited the vehicle and walked into the house. When he got inside, he remained silent until everyone came in. He then commenced passing out choppers to everyone. When he got to the old man, he refused to take a chopper.

"I'm cool wit..." The old man stopped his explanation, smiled, and said, "You'll see."

"Okay, everybody listen up. When we get there. Don't let that nigga leave. Cover all parts of that house."

Lacy's House

"Baby, we can leave now! For real?" Lacy screamed in excitement as Dawg told her they were leaving shortly. He continued making phone calls and closing out his life in Memphis.

"My, my, my! Yes! We're outta this bitch! Memphis is the "city of the dead", but we ain't finna be none of them!" Lacy rushed into her room and started packing a few things that she wanted to take with her, so that she didn't have to buy them again. Although she had more than enough money to do so.

"Erica," Lacy screamed, "Come in here!" Erica had gone to the bathroom.

"Is everything alright?" she asked when she rushed back into the master suite.

"Yeah, I'm leaving this bitch! We outta here."

Erica was shocked at the news. She felt her phone vibrating in her pocket. It was only a text message. She quickly responded to it and continued talking to Lacy. Erica saw another opportunity to live in the house she told Victoria she would one day live in.

"So, what are you gonna do with the house?" she probed.

"Girl, I don't know," Lacy said, as she continued to pack her clothes. She quickly snapped her finger, "You can live here, but whenever I creep back in town, you gotta let me sleep in one of these damn rooms. Hell, you're gonna be in the family anyway," she thought about it, "We'll just set up a payment arrangement, and you can send a little money to me every now and then. The house will remain in my name though. Shit, I would be stupid to get rid of this house, it's prime real estate. We're right off Riverside Dr. girl. The baby is going to love growing up down here."

Erica rushed into Lacy's arms, "Lacy," she cried.

"Girl, stop all that crying," she paused and called for Dawg to come get her bags and take them to the car, "My nephew gon' live in his daddy's house," she smiled because she thought she was doing something nice for a change, "Hell, it was his daddy house, so it's going to be where he lives from now on. Girl, we family."

"No, Lacy. I'm crying because...because…," Erica stuttered as the tears started flooding out of her eyes, "Trap and his crew are on the way."

"NOOO! Erica! What have you done? I've never done anything to you! I just gave you a fuckin' mansion to live in! Why would you do this to me?" Lacy screamed while reaching into her purse to pull out her pistol. She wasted no more time with Erica. She rushed out of the room calling Dawgs' name.

"Dawg! Dawg! Where are you? Don't go out there!" Lacy screamed, but her screams went unheard. She heard the door chime as it was opened and closed.

Outside Lacy's House

Dawg popped the back door on Lacy's Cadillac truck and threw her bags in. He took a deep breath and looked around the downtown community. He never thought that he would have to leave his city to stay alive. He hated to admit it to himself, but he felt like a coward. However, he knew that this was the change he needed. As he headed back to the front door, Lacy came running out calling his name. At the same time, several cars came to a screeching halt in front of the house.

"It's my brother and his crew!" Lacy yelled as both of their eyes locked on the masked men jumping out shooting. Lacy opened fire giving Dawg time to pull his pistol out, "Run, baby!" he instructed Lacy.

Dawg struck out running around the back of the house to hide as Lacy followed behind him. She knew in her heart that Travis had given everybody in his crew strict orders not to shoot his sister. Needless to say, she couldn't tell who the men were. She was shooting at any and everybody with a mask on, at the same time, she was praying that she didn't kill her brother. Little did she know, Travis wasn't wearing a mask. He noticed Dawg running behind the house, so he broke out and ran to the other side. He had been there many times before, therefore he was well acquainted with the property.

"I told you this shit was coming to an end, Dawg!" Travis yelled. From a distance, police sirens could be heard coming towards them. Dawg was going to be saved again, "You one lucky dog. You got more lives than a cat," Travis joked as he was preparing to get out of there before the cops arrived.

"But you don't," Dawg said, standing directly behind Travis with his pistol to his head. "Drop it!" Travis did, and smiled.

"Well played. You got me, now what's the next move? Don't hesitate. I taught you better than that."

"Oh! Nigga you know me. If you weren't my brother, you woulda' been dead by now. I ain't a coward," he said, "Turn around Trap. I told you it didn't have to be like this, but you wouldn't leave well enough alone. And for the record, you ain't TAUGHT me shit! WE learned these streets TOGETHER muthafucka'!" Dawg informed Travis calmly.

"I ain't scared of dying. Just look me in the eye when you pull the trigger. It didn't have to be like this? The fuck you mean nigga? Bitch, you shot my brother!"

"Trap, I ain't fucked up bout killin' you. Now if you will call off the crew and leave me alone, I'll move out of town."

"Kill me nigga. I wanna go see my brother and granny anyway."

Dawg shrugged his shoulders, "Okay, Trap. I love you, but have it your way," POW!... POW! His body collapsed to the pavement with two to the head. Travis looked around and realized that one of his men killed Dawg.

POW!

The body of the hitman that killed Dawg, hit the ground right beside him. He had been shot in the chest and was struggling to live.

"Nooo…" Lacy screamed and rushed over to the dying hitman. She was the shooter that time. She weakly dropped to her knees beside Dawg, "Whyyy Travis? Whyyy?" she screamed up at her twin and beat on the hitman's chest a few times as she cried over Dawg's body. After a few moments, she stood up, looked her brother in the face, and placed her pistol to his head. However, Travis smirked and pointed down at his hitman coughing and fighting for his life.

The man was coughing up so much blood, he could barely speak, but he tried, "I told you that...I," he coughed again and spit out a mouth full of blood, "I… I would be the one to...save...ya' life...again," he slowly removed the mask from his face. It was who he thought it was…his father, Travis Stewart Sr. The old man looked up at his twins and said a silent prayer to God. He asked for enough strength to deliver the last words before he took his final breath. He wanted to talk to the daughter he threw away like trash. God granted him his final wishes and he spoke directly to Lacy.

"Angel Stewart," he coughed, "Your mother loved you! She named you. Look in my left pocket. You'll hear for yourself. I brought the tape with me because I had a funny feeling that I would be trading my life for my son's tonight. If I woulda' been a real father, neither one of you would be standin' here right now. Angel, your granny Laura Mae KNEW you were her granddaughter. That's why she always called you her grandbaby back in Hyde Park. I just refused to tell her the truth! I…am…so sorry! Sooo sorry baby girl," Travis Stewart Sr. started having convulsions and the coughing became uncontrollable as he lost consciousness and closed his eyes forever.

Lacy looked on in shock. Her hand started trembling and she dropped her gun. She realized that she killed her own father, and right before her father spoke up, she had been pointing a pistol to her twin brother's head. She had finally lost all hope.

Travis looked up at Erica standing on the balcony in tears. His heart felt the pain that she was feeling. He knew he had forced her hand because he knew she didn't have anything. He promised her 50 bands. Then he remembered something. Travis bent over and reached into his father's left pocket and found a small recording device. He stared at it confusingly and thought about what his father said. It was for Lacy, so he handed it to her. He looked up at Erica again, nodded, and walked off.

As Travis slowly started to walk towards the side of the house, bullets penetrated his back and right shoulder. His body turned around and hit the ground. He gasped for air.

In unison, Lacy and Erica screamed, "Noooo!!!"

The shooter walked over to Travis' body and stared down at him, "I told you I was going to get ya' black ass! Die muthafucka! Die," the man screamed, as he looked at Travis. Travis recognized the voice and quickly focused in on the face. It was Captain Reid, and he was out of uniform. Travis rested his head back on the concrete because he knew at that moment, the Captain had gone rogue. He also knew the Captain was about to put more bullets in him, so he said a quick prayer and closed his eyes.

POW!... POW!... POW!

Captain Reid's body dropped next to Travis. The rookie cop rushed over and shot the Captain three times in the head. Unbeknownst to everyone but Travis, the rookie had been on his payroll for months. The sirens that were heard in the distance were from the rookie's car only. He had overheard Captain Reid making plans to kill Travis the day before, so he rushed to the scene to make sure that didn't happen. From the looks of it, he was too late. As the rookie tried to figure out his next move, he heard the radio from his police car informing him that several other cars had been dispatched since his arrival, and they were on their way.

He leaned over to Travis and nervously said, "I tried to call you, but you didn't answer," he placed his arms under his body to pick him up, "One of you guys help me," he yelled to members of Travis' crew, "I gotta get him away from here and to the hospital. Quick!"

"No hospital. Call Dr. Morris. She fucks with us," Travis informed the rookie.

Lacy stood by as they picked up her brother and carried him away. She overheard one of the men say, "Fuck! This nigga ain't gon' make it!" she sat on the ground next to Dawg and held his hand while staring at the small recorder. She could no longer think straight, she was slowly losing her mind.

"The itsy-bitsy spider went up the water spout…" the nursery rhyme that drove Victoria over the edge of her own balcony, was summoning Lacy. She looked up at the balcony and saw Erica, but she started hallucinating and pictured Victoria hanging from the rail. She then started humming the nursery rhyme as she stood up and walked towards the Mississippi River.

Chapter 13

LAKESIDE

****2 Months Later****

Two months earlier, Lacy was found getting ready to walk into the Mississippi River to drown herself. She no longer wanted to live. The memories of her loved ones drove her to the water. Travis was dead, Dawg was dead, her baby brother; Luther, was dead, all of her parents had died violently, and she was torn about pulling the trigger on her own father. In addition to losing most of her family, she remembered the only grandmother she had ever known was a distant, painful memory. Lacy cried as she thought of her granny Laura Mae because she knew if she were alive, she could run to her with all of her burdens. She had no one left on earth to live for. However, before the current swept her away, her only living sibling; Chris, ran into the water and saved her. He had been keeping an even closer watch on her since the day Luther died.

The day the shooting started at Luther and Victoria's old home, he left the scene and prayed that Lacy wouldn't get hit in the crossfire. However, he didn't go far. He went down on the river and tried to wait until the shooting stopped. And when it did, he was about to make his way back towards the house to check on Lacy, but noticed her proceeding to walk off the river bank right into the water. The strong currents were sure to take her away. Chris panicked and raced down to save her just in the nick of time. Needless to say, several undercovers were down there trying to keep the young teens away because of the pandemic, and they witnessed him pulling her away from the water. Chris tried to tell them that he would take care of

her, but they wouldn't listen. They told him they had to follow the proce-
dure for a suicide attempt.

The undercover officers took her to Lakeside Mental Hospital to have
her evaluated. After the evaluation, they admitted her. She was diagnosed
with bipolar disorder, schizophrenia, and depression. They refused to allow her to leave until she got the proper care she needed. Unfortunately,
even with the power that the Walker family possessed, Chris was unable
to get them to release her. He had found out that his adopted sister was no
stranger to Lakeside Mental Hospital. She had been admitted as a teenager,
and his aunt; Elizabeth Walker, was able to have her released into her custody. However, this time, the psychiatrist said that Lacy needed to remain
in the facility for her own safety.

As the doctors and nurses administered meds and made sure Lacy attended
her therapy sessions daily, they started to see some improvement in her
behavior. She was not talking about killing herself as often, so they were
happy about that. They were also finally able to locate a small battery to
play the old tape recorder that Lacy's dad had wanted her to hear. The day
she listened to it was the roughest day of her life.

"Ok Lacy, we got it working. And just so you'll know, it is policy that I
listen to whatever my patients listen to first. So, I've listened to this recording, and I have to tell you though, it is very clear, but it is heartbreaking.
Are you sure you want to hear this?" the therapist asked.

"Yes! I'm ready. I wanna hear my mama!"

The therapist pushed play on the recorder and walked to the other side
of the room. She wanted Lacy to have a little privacy.

As Lacy listened to the recording of the night her biological father;
Travis Stewart Sr. sold her to her white parents, her emotions were all over
the place. She heard a side of her adopted father; Christopher, she never
knew existed. He was crazy and so was her real father. The more she listened, the better she felt about killing her father a few months before. In

the recording, he seemed to have had no guilt about selling her to strangers for drugs. The part of the tape that made her smile, but also ripped her heart in half was when her mother's voice boomed through the tiny speaker…

"Give me my fucking child! Give me my baby! That's MY baby. That's MY Angel. PLEASE! SOMEBODY HELP ME! They takin' my baby!" she screamed to everyone in the Exxon parking lot that was watching the scene unfold, "What the fuck is wrong with you people? The man in the red car! The red-headed white bitch! They got my child! Big T, you lettin' them take our baby! We got 2 babies! We got twins! I KNOW I had 2! God help me! I'm sorry God! Father God Almighty! Please! I know I ain't the best wife or daughter, and I ain't been a good Christian either, but if you give me a chance, I promise to be the best mama lil Travis and Angel has ever seen. Please God! Give me a chance! I ain't gotta smoke no more! No more crack for me God! I'm done with the Heroin, Cocaine, Lortabs, Xanax, Ecstasy, Opium, Pcp, Lsd, Bath Salts, Marijuana, Percocet's, Cough Syrup, and oh yeah God…Laundry Detergent!"

Lacy listened to her mother begging her adopted father; Christopher, and her aunt Hannah to not take her. She also felt her mother's pain when she confessed her addiction to so many drugs. Her mother was sick, and Lacy's heart went out to her. She thought about her grandmother Laura Mae's funeral, and how her mother; Mary, was trying to touch her, but she would not allow her to. At the time, she did not know that was her mother.

"Ohhh mama! I didn't know! I just didn't know!" Lacy screamed in her room and cried harder than she had ever cried in her life. She suddenly missed the mother she never knew.

For the rest of that night, Lacy replayed the recording at least twenty-five more times. Eventually, the therapist sent word to the nurses for them to confiscate the recorder because it was causing Lacy to regress.

A few days later, nurses and counselors were in and out of Lacy's room for various reasons, and they all observed her sitting in the corner of her room. Just as she always did, she was singing *The Itsy-Bitsy-Spider* song. Unfortunately, they failed to notice that each time the door opened; she moved closer to it. Around noon, one of the nurses entered her room to give her a dose of medicine.

"Lacy, baby it's time to take your medicine," the nurse said, as she told her to open her mouth wide. Lacy continued to sing her song. The nurse started singing with her. She knew that was the only way to get her to take her meds. That had been an ongoing thing for the past two months, "Lacy, you know I want you to get well so you can go home and be with your brother. He comes to see you every day. But you never talk to him."

"I talked to Travis a few minutes ago," Lacy said, as she drooled.

"No, not Travis. Your other brother."

"Travis, is the only one that has been here," she started screaming, and the orderlies came rushing in. They gave her a shot to sedate her, and she immediately laid on the cold floor.

"Poor baby. She loves this Travis guy. Does anybody know who he is?"

"Yeah, he was a drug dealer that got shot by the police twice," the male nurse stated.

"Did he live?" she asked.

"From what I've heard of that night, it didn't look good for him."

"That's the only person she talks about, but Chris is the name of the guy that comes to visit her every day."

Malaysia's Car

Kesha jumped into the passenger's side of Malaysia's Rolls Royce before she pulled out of the grocery store lot. As she sat and ignored Malaysia's gray-eyed glare, she admired the luxury. She had to admit, she was impressed. Kesha rubbed the soft leather and touched the wide screen tv while nodding her head in approval of the dark purple truck.

"Yeah, this shit is nice," she looked at Malaysia and locked evil eyes with her. She then slid her pistol out of her pocket, "I think you've been dodging me. You owe me a mill ticket, and I came to collect. And don't even think about telling me you ain't got my money," Kesha paused as she looked around the lot.

"Kesha, do you think I ride around with a million dollars on me? No!"

"Bitch, don't get smart. Because I will kill ya' ass right here," Kesha showed her the pistol, "Where the fuck is my money? I didn't tell Trap shit!"

"Well Trap is...,"

"Bitch, if you say it, you die!" she threatened, "Now, for the last time, let's go get my muthafuckin' money, BITCH!"

"Okay, okay. Calm down. You can follow me to my crib."

"Naw, hoe. I'm riding with you. I'll catch an Uber back to my shit.

Malaysia's House

Kesha and Malaysia walked into her home, and Malaysia told Kesha to make herself comfortable, "Let me go upstairs to get it."

"I don't trust you. I'ma go with you. And that's crazy as shit that you got that type of money up in here. If I was still into robbin' and kickin' in doors like when I was younger, I woulda' loved a nice lil hit like this! But, nah mane. You lead the way, you might call the police," Malaysia walked up the steps, and Kesha walked behind her staring at her ass. She couldn't resist herself, so she reached up and squeezed it, "You got a fat ass too. I see why Trap was in love with that ass. Bet that pussy good too."

Malaysia looked back and said, "Was... Hmph! Yes, it was good to him. And wouldn't you like to know?"

"I sure would," Kesha answered.

They reached the top of the steps, and Malaysia went into a private room. She moved a full-length mirror on the wall revealing a hidden safe. Kesha watched the entire time. She pointed her gun at Malaysia's back.

"Kesha, why is your gun pointed at me?"

"Bitch, how many times do I have to tell you I... DON'T... TRUST... YOU."

She opened the safe quickly and reached in to get the bag she already had set to the side for Kesha.

"Here you go. Now you can go up the street and catch the bus, call an Uber, or walk. I don't give a fuck. Just leave my house and never come back."

"Sure thing, 'Ms. Good Pussy'," Kesha turned to leave, but turned back around, "Oh yeah, I hate to tell you this, but I did tell Trap," she laughed, "I had to. On the ride to kill Dawg, it wasn't sitting right with me. I have always been a loyal bitch. I would never do anything to hurt my baby."

"Baby?" Malaysia laughed, "He would never fuck with someone like you."

"You think?" she shrugged her shoulders, "Oh well, but I had to get this money though."

"So what? You told him. What can he do now?"

"Even now, he's still running shit. He told me to tell you…BYE!"

"Huh?"

"BYE BITCH!" Kesha shouted, as she unloaded four shots to Malaysia's chest, "What makes you think he wouldn't fuck wit' me? Hoe, he fucked me long before he fucked you. And I made sure he enjoyed it," Kesha laughed to herself and walked back over to the safe to get the rest of the money. She reached deeper into the safe, pulled out an envelope, and hugged it.

"Yep…It's mine… mine… mine!" she excitedly jumped up and down and then called her clean-up crew to dispose of the body. Never to be found, "Today was a good day. And things are about to get better," she said out loud, as she rushed down the steps and grabbed the keys to her new car off the hook near the garage door. She then got behind the wheel of the dark purple Rolls Royce Cullinan and backed out of the driveway.

Chapter 14

HAPPILY EVER AFTER

The big day had finally come for her. She thought it would never happen in her lifetime. All her life she had been the one that thought she was the girl that guys only wanted to fuck. Sure, she was beautiful and had a nice body, but wifey material, she never thought it. There she stood in the full-length mirror admiring her dress. She looked stunning in her white-lace Vera Wang wedding gown. Her hair was on point. Her nails and toes were well manicured, not to mention the six-inch stilettos, with the diamond straps on them. They accentuated the four-karat diamond earrings that dangled from her ears. Tears slowly trickled down her face, as she sat down on the bed. Her emotions were all over the place.

"I don't deserve this," she cried, "He'll never love me the way I've loved him."

"Don't say that, sis. You deserve it just as much as anyone else," she took a deep breath, "And I know for a fact he's gon' love you. It's your big day. You're supposed to be happy. Smile."

"I guess. Maybe I'm just scared. I don't want to go back to…"

"Stop it," her sister chimed in, "You look gorgeous. And he loves you, "You truly deserve this. It's been a long time coming. Now, get ya' panties out the bunch, and let's go get you married."

"Wait, sis," she stood and looked her directly in the eyes, "I don't have on any panties," they laughed and left the room.

The church was filled to capacity as everyone made their way inside. Chairs were placed in the aisle just to accommodate the overflow of guests.

Flowers lined the front of the church, as rose petals were sprinkled through-out on the floor. Some of Memphis' own celebrities came to show support. Yo Gotti, Black Youngsta, MoneyBagg Yo, and Split Personality all lined the left side of the room, as Young Dolph, Three 6 Mafia, 8 Ball & MJG filled in the seats on the right. Brian McKnight was singing all of his hits as the guests walked in.

Kesha made it to the entrance of the sanctuary, and her eyes lit up like a Christmas tree. She couldn't believe her eyes. She looked at her sister and said, "I'm nervous and scared. All these people came out to support us?"

"Yes! The music is playing. We gots to go," her sister kissed her on the cheek and walked in ahead of her. She was the Maid of Honor.

When she was able to look down the aisle and see her love, she couldn't contain herself. The man she had loved since she was a young girl was fi-nally standing there looking good enough to eat. Although he was holding himself up with a cane, she didn't care. She had her man.

She walked down the aisle and started crying as everyone admired her beauty. At the front of the church, the man of her dreams stood on his golden cane waiting for his beautiful wife-to-be. As he stood there, he thought back to the moment he realized that she was the one.

****Two Months Earlier****

"Look, I know I said don't worry about it, but I gots to keep it 100 with you," she paused and took a deep breath, "When we were at the hospital, and I went out in the hall, I had stolen Malaysia's diary and read it. Here, look at this," she passed him her iPhone and showed him what she discov-ered, "I screenshotted it before she had a chance to catch me. This is the real reason baby Laura-Anne was in the hospital," she watched his facial expression, "I couldn't dare let you marry that bitch knowing your child's life would be in this bitch hands when you ain't there. She offered me money not to tell you. Now I'm not saying that she don't love you, but that bitch got a few screws missing, not loose, but missing," Travis took it all in and immediately made a phone call.

"Hey, Nell. Where you at? I need you to do something for me," he listened for her response, "Cool. I need you to go down to Lebonheur and go to room 212. Tell Laysia that I said Laura-Anne is supposed to go with you when they discharge her in a little while. Make sure you get the car seat out of Malaysia's car, and can you keep her until in the morning for me? If you got something to do, take her to aunt Kay Kay's house. She got milk and shit over there already," he listened to his cousin agree to help him out, "Aight! Listen, IF, for whatever reason, something happens to me, I need Lacy to get Erica's baby when it gets here, and Kesha gon' raise Laura-Anne," he looked at Kesha lovingly while pulling the phone away from his ear. Nell was yelling through the phone because she didn't agree with him about who would raise Laura-Anne, "Calm down cuz! Trust me on this, Kesha gon' do right by my baby. I'm sure of it! And I need y'all to help both her and Lacy out with the kids. Please do that for ya' boy. Money is no problem. Between me and Dre's assets put together, we got over 10 million. Plus, neither Lacy nor Kesha need any money, they both good!" he listened as Nell asked a thousand questions about Kesha, "Mane," he laughed, "I will tell you in the morning. Now please, go get my baby from that triflin' bitch!" he hung up and looked back at Kesha.

"Let's get this situation over with, and we can go from there," he smiled at her and said thank you, "You always looking out for me. And please believe me, I see you. Don't think I don't. I see everything you have done and doing," he leaned over and kissed her on the lips, but quickly pulled away.

Kesha's heart skipped a beat because she was positive that her love for him was always real. Beyond the street life and random sex. It was true love. However, neither one of them ever showed it.

"Kesha, if what you sayin' is true. Whether I live or die, go get your money, and kill that bitch. And when you do, get it all. Don't leave a dime. And the car. She keeps the title near the money. I want you to live like a queen. Get married, have kids, and take care of my daughter. As you just heard, Lacy gon' take Erica's son for me. But make sure y'all work together on that shit because I want them to be raised close, like me and Dre' used to be. I don't trust Erica's greedy, hoe ass to raise my nephew. He ain't gon' be no street nigga like me, so she can come around, but she know what it is. And tell Lacy that I said, if he starts being a money-hungry asshole like his daddy, beat the shit outta him. Don't spare the rod not one gotdamn time! He gon' be a humble lil nigga. I do NOT want another Dre' runnin' around here," he laughed as tears formed in his eyes. Kesha had an eerie feeling deep down in the pit of her stomach that this would be their last time together.

"Trap, I got you. You're gonna be alright. I promise. I'll die for you," she cried. They gave each other dap and said in unison, "Let's get this shit done. By any means necessary."

Present Day

As she made it to the altar, Travis switched his cane to his right hand and allowed her to take hold of his left arm. She looked him in the eyes and said I love you. She thought back to the day he was rushed to the hospital.

Two Months Earlier

Speeding down Riverside Dr. to get to Dr. Morris' condo, Kesha held onto Travis like never before, "Come on, Trap. Breathe baby, breathe. I can't lose you. We just got started! Breathe, Trap Breathe!"

She cried, as the rookie cop turned his flashing lights on to force everyone to move out of his way. He had to do his part to help save Travis' life. He had been taking real good care of the rookie, financially, and he didn't want that to stop.

"Hurry!" Kesha yelled at the rookie and beat on the back of his seat, "Stay with me, Trap, we here baby! Stay with me!"

Travis opened his eyes and tried to talk as more blood spewed out of his mouth, "Kesha, it's...alright," she smiled, "If it's my… time… it's my…" his head dropped to the side as he passed out from the loss of too much blood.

"NOOO!" Kesha screamed, "Trap, I love you. Please don't leave me!"

****Present Day****

Kesha stood at the altar trembling because she was staring into the eyes of the love of her life. Before the preacher could start the ceremony, she leaned over and kissed him. Everyone laughed.

"I guess she couldn't wait!" the preacher joked, and everyone laughed. The ceremony began.

"Do you, Kesha Jackson, take Travis Stewart Jr. to be your lawfully wedded husband, to cherish, to love, to obey, through sickness and health, and forsake all others for the rest of your life?"

"Yep, I shol' do. Yes sir, Mr. Preacher man. I shol' do. Now, come on! Hurry this up!" again, she leaned over and gave him a kiss. The people erupted in laughter again.

"Well, at least we know this one is going to last. She clearly loves him," more laughter filled the room, "And do you Travis Stewart Jr., take Kesha Jackson to be your lawfully wedded wife, to love, and to cherish, through sickness and health, and forsake all others, for the rest of your life?"

"Yep, he do," Kesha answered for him and everyone laughed.

"Ms. Jackson, he has to say it," the preacher said to Kesha.

She looked at Travis and he smiled, "You heard her! What she said."

"Is that a yes?" the preacher asked for clarity.

"I do." Travis said.

"By the power vested in me, I now pronounce you husband and wife," the preacher looked at Kesha, "You may NOW, kiss your husband."

Kesha leaned in and shoved her tongue down Travis' throat, and they kissed passionately for so long that the preacher had to break it up.

Cheers could be heard throughout the sanctuary as everyone stood to their feet and cheered.

A young kid came and laid a broom down in front of them. They looked at each other, counted to three, and jumped over the broom.

"Everyone! I proudly present to you, Mr., and Mrs. Travis Stewart Jr." the preacher announced, and the church went wild in excitement for the new couple.

Outside, a stretch limo was awaiting the new Stewart family to transport them to the reception in The Grand Ballroom of the Peabody Hotel. Travis walked out slowly on his cane and motioned for his aunt Kay Kay to hand him his daughter. Expertly, he balanced baby Laura-Anne with one arm. As they were preparing to get in the limo, a car full of girls drove down the street screaming congratulations, as they hung out the window showing their breasts to Travis. Kesha placed her hands over his eyes, however; one girl popped out of the sunroof and commenced shooting at him. It was obvious that she was trying to kill him and his daughter. With a quick reaction, Kesha pulled Travis and the baby down into the limo and pulled her 9mm from underneath her wedding dress. She came up shooting. She realized who it was. She hit the back windshield of the shooter's car, shattering the glass as she continued to shoot out the back tires. The car crashed into a nearby pole. Kesha reloaded and headed straight for the car.

Travis laid the baby on the backseat and screamed for his cousin Nell to get in the limo with her. Everyone else had either run back into the church or found safety elsewhere. He limped over to the crashed car behind his wife. He wanted to know who wanted him dead bad enough to do it at a church. It couldn't have been one of Dawg's men. He thought to himself. As Kesha approached the car, she saw Tameka reaching for the pistol that she dropped on the floor during the crash.

"Tameka? I knew we should have killed ya' ass that day at granny's house," Kesha shot Tameka in the hand, and she screamed out in agony, "Go head, hoe. Reach for it again!"

Travis finally made it to the car. When he saw Tameka, he instantly regretted not killing her the day of Kita's murder.

"Fuck you, Trap!" she screamed and held her bleeding hand, "What, you thought I wasn't gon' get that money?"

"What money?" he asked.

"Dawg told his aunt Jackie to contact me if he died. He wanted you dead nigga, and he told her to pay me."

"Bitch, I gave you an opportunity to live! Now you can go tell Dawg in person I said, 'Never send a money hungry hoe, to kill a killer.' She will never get it done. You were too sloppy, bitch."

One of the other girls in the car pleaded for her life, "I promise, Trap, on God. We didn't know what she was about to do. She told us to drive by, so she could say goodbye before you left for the reception, Trap. I put that on God."

Travis shook his head, "Why does everybody lie on God?" at that moment, Kesha and Travis unloaded a tyrant of bullets on everybody in the car. They looked back at the few wedding guests that were bold enough to linger around and then at the rookie cop. He rushed over to involve himself in the slaughter, in order to protect his money, Travis. He fired a few rounds into the car, as an act of self-defense.

"Go on, Trap, leave. I got this. It was all in self-defense. I'll handle it from here. I got promoted. I'm the new Captain," he winked and called the incident in.

The Great Escape

Lacy was sitting in the television room conversing with one of the nurses as she did her hair. She looked amazing and was happy because she was finally starting to look like her old self. Anyone that walked in, and didn't know that she was a patient, easily mistook her for one of the nurses. She knew then that the time had come for her to vacate the premises.

"Nurse Willis, do you mind if I go take a shower?" asked Lacy.

"Sure, let me get you some clean clothes.

Lacy went into the restroom and started taking a shower. She was well aware that they weren't allowed to be alone, so she had to take a quick shower and be ready to get dressed when the nurse returned.

As Nurse Willis entered the shower area, she called out Lacy's name, "Lacy, you can come out now," she said with a pleasant tone, "I have you some fresh clothes to put on," she looked at the clothes, "These are nice. Somebody brought you some nice clothes," she took a few more steps and fell to the ground. Lacy hit her across the head with her fist, stripped her of her clothes, and pulled her into the shower. She quickly put on Nurse Willis' scrubs, hat, I.D, and took her keys. She headed for the door and wasted no time walking out. No one even gave her a second look. As soon as she got outside the doors, she pushed the panic button on the remote control to find Nurse Willis' car.

When she heard the loud beeping sound, she whispered to herself, "There it is," and Lacy ran like lightning towards it, "I won't be going back in there ever again. I'm going home," she jumped in the car and sped off, *"The itsy bitsy spider went up the water spout…"* she sang over and over again until she made it downtown to Monteigne Dr., "Home at last," she quietly opened the door and crept upstairs. She heard loud music playing as she made her way into the Media Room.

There, she spotted Erica laying back on the chaise with her eyes closed, rubbing her big belly, sipping on a glass of red wine. She slowly walked over to her and stood in front of her as she swayed her head from side to side. She couldn't help but to slap the shit out of her.

Slap! Erica's eyes popped open, as red wine flew across the room. The sight of Lacy nearly made her piss on herself. She stood up and backed up just a little to gather herself.

"La.. Lacy. How are you? I tried to come…"

"Bitch, save the lies. You ain't tried to come do shit!" Lacy walked closer, "I gave you this," she twirled around in a circle, "Lovely home to live in, and hoe you sold me out. All we wanted to do was leave town! But ya' money hungry ass had to call my crazy ass brother," she got even closer, "I'm a fuckin' STEWART. I'm his twin, so we think just alike," Lacy's eyes widened, "Do you know what I'm thinkin'?" Erica shook her head no, "Well, bitch, let me tell you. Somebody is gonna die in here today," again, she slapped Erica, "Come on hoe, follow me, so I can show you who."

Erica nervously followed her, at the same time holding her stomach in fear.

Lacy walked into the master suite, grabbed a sheet, walked to the balcony, and tied one end to the railing. She went back and got another one to do the same thing.

"Bring ya' ass over here now!" she yelled.

"No, Lacy, I'm carrying your brother's child."

Lacy laughed at Erica's begging, "Which brother? They both been fuckin' the same bitches all their life, so which one? Luther or Travis?" she paused, "You better say the right name," Lacy threatened as she smiled like the Joker. The expression on her face was sinister. Death was written all over her.

Frightened, Erica said, "Travis! It's Travis baby!"

"Wrong answer!" shouted Lacy, "He helped my father kill my man!"

"I meant it's Luther. Luther's baby. You got me scared, Lacy," she continued to cry.

"Wrong answer again. He saw me get raped and did nothing. He hated me. So, I hate him," she wrapped her arm around Erica and smiled, "Next, you were gonna say it was my daddy's baby weren't you? I knew you were a nasty bitch!"

Lacy forcefully moved Erica closer to the balcony railing.

Chris

Chris sat outside Lacy's house wondering if he should go knock on the door or leave. He knew the police were on their way. An hour before he got to Monteigne Dr., he had arrived at Lakeside for his daily visit, and when he asked to see Lacy, they couldn't find her. However, they did find Nurse Willis still knocked out and stripped down to her panties and bra in the shower. They also discovered that the nurse's car had been stolen. Chris shook his head when he thought about the trouble he would be in if they thought he helped her escape. Since he made initial contact with his sister, he had already helped her to return a kidnapped baby and saved her from walking into the Mississippi River. He was starting to think that Lacy was more trouble than he was willing to put up with. He wasn't built for the life of crime and drama like she was.

"Fuck you Lacy! The more I help you the more you get ya' ass in trouble," he yelled inside his car and stepped out to walk towards the door. As he got ready to knock on the door, he realized that it was cracked, "Lacy," Chris whispered, "Lacy, this Chris," slowly, he pushed the door open and walked in. He heard two voices that sounded like they were arguing. He decided to follow the voices to find out who was in the house with Lacy. First, he located the kitchen and grabbed a knife, then he cautiously followed the sounds of the commotion upstairs, "Lord, please be with me. I'm not ready to die," again, he called out to his sister, "Lacy!"

He finally reached the top of the stairs and overheard an unfamiliar voice seemingly begging Lacy not to hurt her. He quietly stood near the doorway to the master suite and listened.

"Lacy, please don't do this to your nephew. I'm pregnant. Look at me," Erica cried.

"You got one around your neck, and I got one around my neck," she held on to Erica's hand tightly, "You helped them kill my man. So, why don't we go together to see him. You can apologize to him then. I hope you don't get hot too easily because I know Dawg is in hell for all the shit he did. Oh! And while we're down there, we get to see Luther, Travis, and Victoria too. We're going to have a big reunion! Yayyy!"

Out of desperation, Erica took a chance to see if she could change Lacy's mind.

"Lacy, Trap ain't dead. He just married Kesha."

"Stop lying. Why would he marry her? She was just work-for-hire."

"No, I'm not lying. Kesha killed Malaysia because she tried to kill Laura-Anne," Erica explained.

"My brother is alive!" anger rushed her, "My man's murderer gets to walk around breathing and even get married, and I don't have anyone left to love me? He gotta go too! Travis must die!"

Chris walked into the room and called out to her, "Lacy, sis. What are you doing? Stop it," he calmly moved closer to her, "You don't have to do this. Come on sis, we must go. The police are on the way. I got to get you outta here. The nurse's car has a GPS tracker on it," Chris moved closer to her and her mind went blank. And then she realized that she was standing in the same spot Victoria was standing in when she killed herself.

"No, I don't want to," Lacy yelled, facing the balcony rail. She was looking out at the M-Bridge, "No, I don't want to sing it anymore," at that moment, she didn't realize that she took her arms away from Erica.

"Lacy," Chris said, "Who are you talking to?" he moved closer to Erica and cut the sheet from around her neck with the knife. Erica was so scared she was frozen in place. She couldn't move, so she watched Chris desperately trying to save his sister. He knew Lacy was hallucinating.

"I'm talking to Vicki, lil brother," she turned back around and started talking to herself again, "Vicki, I'm sorry. I never meant to hurt you," Lacy was talking as if she were filled with Thorazine. She started to drool at the mouth, "Do you forgive me, Vicki?" Lacy pretended to be dancing with someone, "You want me to come visit you? You do. Okay, here I come," Lacy stood on the rail as Chris tried to talk her down.

"Lacy!" he screamed, "Sis, get down from there. You can't go visit her; she is not here."

"Chris, yes she is. She's standing right next to me," she looked to the right of her and smiled, "Okay, you want me to sing with you. Chris, she wants all of us to sing a song. *The itsy- bitsy-spider went up the water spout. Down came the rain and washed the spider out, out came the sun…*" she paused and looked at Erica, "Bitch, why you not singing? I'ma get down from here and choke the…" Lacy lost her balance as her foot slipped off the rail and she went over the balcony. The sheet was not tied properly, so it came loose from the railing, and she hit the ground below.

"NOOO…" Chris ran down the steps and out of the house yelling for Erica to call an ambulance. When he made it to the walk path behind the house, he saw Lacy's body sprawled out on the sidewalk. He kneeled beside her and checked her pulse, to his surprise, she was still alive. Tears were rolling down her face as she told him she couldn't feel anything in her body. He knew she was paralyzed. The nerves in her spinal cord were damaged. Chris held her hand until the ambulance arrived.

The paramedics started working on her immediately. They slid her body onto a wooden board and then onto the stretcher. They were trying to keep her back as straight as possible. It was broken. She had suffered severe back and neck injuries. Chris and Erica stood by in silence. When one of the paramedics asked if he wanted to ride to the hospital with Lacy, he said he would.

"Ok. I'm coming!" he jumped into the ambulance and before they closed the doors, he realized that all of the fun things he wanted to do with his big sister would never happen. Life as she once knew it was over.

3 Months Later

Lacy was finally released from the hospital in a wheelchair. Chris had been by his sister's side every day, so when she was discharged, he was happy to pick her up. Travis, his wife; Kesha, along with their babies, Laura-Anne and lil Dre' sat in their Rolls Royce truck in the far back of the hospital parking lot. They watched as Chris pushed Lacy to his van. Due to her fragile mental state, her psychiatrist told him that she needed a few weeks to adjust before she could be around Travis. She felt that seeing him would bring back too many bad memories from the night Dawg was killed, so Chris was doing most of the work when it came to their sister.

Travis and Chris had met with each other the month before, and they both agreed to get her the best rehab doctors in the world. Due to her condition, she couldn't live alone. Travis also knew he couldn't take care of her because Kesha was pregnant, and it had been so rough on her that she could barely take care of Laura-Anne and lil Dre'. So, he was taking care of both of his kids by himself and running all of his businesses at the same time. Fortunately, money was not an issue for Travis or Chris, they just wanted her to get the care she needed. They both loved her and wanted the best for her, so Chris willingly accepted the responsibility of taking care of her, and the plan was for her to live with him in River Oaks.

Chris opened the door to the new wheelchair accessible van, by Mercedes Benz that Travis bought for him. He wanted him to be able to move her around without having to pick her up. He wanted everything to be as easy and stress free as possible for Chris. He had also arranged for around the clock caretakers so that Chris could still enjoy his young life. He was only 20 years old.

As the automated door was closing, Lacy shook her head in sadness and allowed the tears to fall. She tried again to move her arms, and although she knew it was pointless, she refused to stop torturing herself. Chris turned the ignition and sympathetically watched his sister cry soft tears at her new way of living. Paralyzed from her shoulders down, he knew the road ahead was going to be a difficult one for her.

"Don't cry, Lacy. I got you," assured Chris.

"Bruh, I killed my daddy and he deserved it! My mama loved me. She didn't want to sell me for no drugs! She was sick! My own daddy did that to me!" tears poured down her face.

"Yes, your mama Mary really did love you sis! And your daddy was sick too! He didn't know what he was doing. But, our mama and daddy loved you too remember?" they rode in silence for a few minutes until Lacy spoke again.

"Yeah, mama and daddy Blake loved me too. I love them. Chris, where are we going?" she asked in a tone that was barely audible.

"Home. Lacy, you're finally going back to your happy place," he responded.

"River Oaks?" she asked with hope.

"Yes. Home to River Oaks," he smiled warmly.

"Finally," she smiled and stared out the window as Chris drove down Walnut Grove. However, her feelings for Travis were still in limbo. She didn't know if she wanted to love him or hate him. But in her mind, she was saying, *"Travis must die."*

Chris was about to turn the radio on but stopped when he heard Lacy humming a familiar nursery rhyme. He looked over at her, and she was staring directly at him. Strangely, she seemed to be singing the song to him. A mysterious feeling knocked at his soul, but because the song appeared to be relaxing to her, he decided to sing along...

The itsy-bitsy spider... went up the water spout... down came the rain and washed the spider out...

THE END.

THE TANGLED IN A LOVER'S WEB SERIES IN CHRONOLOGICAL ORDER

BOOK 1

TANGLED IN A
Lover's
WEB
MURDER, SEX, LIES, AND DARK SECRETS
B'SHONE & CHINA

BOOK 2: PREQUEL

BOOK 3: PREQUEL
From Tangled in a Lover's Web: The Novel
Penhandler's Ink
She's too
black
to be white
and too
white
to be black
LACY
Caviar to Collard Greens
CHINA

BOOK 4

HYDE PARK Ink
Penhandler's Ink
PRESENTS
TANGLED IN A
Lover's Web 2
THE COLLAPSED WEB
B'SHONE & CHINA

AUTHOR BIO

B'SHONE

B'Shone was born in Memphis, Tennessee and raised on the "shawt" end of the Hyde Park neighborhood, in North Memphis. He graduated from Fairley High School and attended Lincoln University in Jefferson City, Missouri, and Lemoyne-Owen College, in Memphis, Tennessee.

As a young man, B'Shone developed a love for Street Literature and became a major fan. It was not long before he realized that many of the stories he was reading, were similar to his

real-life experiences. With this in mind, he decided to throw his hat in the ring and enter the world of Urban Fiction. He became a "penhandler" and started hustling his writing talents, by putting his knowledge of street life and his ability to create compelling stories to the test. His hard work and determination were manifested in his first literary efforts: *Wrong Side of the Lake* and *Everybody Wants Her*. A few years later, he followed those extraordinary stories with the unforgettable series: *Tangled in a Lover's Web*. His books in that series are: *Tangled in a Lover's Web 1, B'Shone... How It All Starts, Tangled in a Lover's Web 2: Collapsed Web,* and *Dawg vs. Travis: Smoking Web*.

In addition to writing, B'Shone publishes and promotes up and coming authors through his publishing company: Hyde Park Ink and is dedicated to introducing new writing talent to the world.

Currently, B'Shone resides in Memphis, Tennessee, and when he is not writing, or reviewing writing submissions from future authors, he spends his time ministering and motivating children to pursue their dreams.

He is also a licensed barber who selflessly gives his time, talents, and money to the Elderly and others in need.